Houseman's Wager

by
Cathy Linton

MAGNA PRINT BOOKS
Long Preston, North Yorkshire,
England.

British Library Cataloguing in Publication Data.

_____

Linton, Cathy
  Houseman's wager.
  I. Title
  823'.914 (F)   PR6062.I5/

  ISBN 1-85057-157-0
  ISBN 1-85057-158-9 Pbk

First Published in Great Britain 1980

Published in Large Print 1987 by arrangement with the copyright holder.

Printed and bound in Great Britain by
Redwood Burn Limited, Trowbridge, Wiltshire.

CHAPTER ONE

It was a generally accepted fact among those best qualified to judge such things—and a certain young doctor named Jamie McTweed had no hesitation in including himself in this category—that St Lawrence's Hospital, Titchford, turned out not only the most efficient, capable and highly trained nurses in the country but also by far the prettiest.

To be strictly accurate, of course, it did not actually *turn them out*. Rather, it cherished, nurtured and generally clasped them to its stony bosom, ostensibly to ensure the adequate skilled staffing of its wards, theatres and departments: in reality, of course, solely for the admiration, delectation and delight of every doctor, student and other red-blooded male within a ten-mile radius...better make that a fifty-mile radius remembering the long warm summer evenings, the fast roads round Titchford and the number of long low sports cars about— preferably the bright-coloured ones about two inches off the ground, open and making the noise of a dragon gargling when they travel.

Gently loosen the tongue of any healthy young medic or similar red-blooded male in the area—the aforementioned Jamie McTweed on both counts, for instance, or any of his drinking companions at the White Rabbit— and after say, two or three unaccustomed shorts or a few pints of best bitter a distant look would come into their eyes and, in terms guaranteed to stir the tardiest blood, they would compare the beauties, assets, talents and potential availabilities or otherwise of such past and present stars in the Larry's firmament as Gina Mitchell, the scrumptious blonde ex-Casualty sister with the china-doll looks and the knack of appearing bandbox fresh no matter what carnage raged round her, who had set countless male hearts pounding at breakneck speed under their string vests; or Jackie Coles, and that black bathing costume she used to wear, half French, ooh-la-la, and oozing sex appeal as naturally as most people breathe; or Susannah Campbell, nursing gold medallist of her year, looking every inch a champion, a classy filly if ever there was one but as highly-strung as a circus pony; and if it was temperament you liked, what about that fiery little redhead, Jenny What's-her-name, who used to be engaged to one of the doctors at the hospital but ended up marrying an accountant and settling down as domesticated as you please...

What about that bouncy little Swedish auxiliary nurse on outpatients, or that raven-haired second-year raver on the neuro. theatre with such a reputation for keeping herself to herself that it was difficult even to find out what her name was...

There were less glamorous girls around

too, naturally, whose talents, although undeniable, were less in evidence. Even Larry's, enlightened as it was, had not reached the stage of making good looks a prerequisite for admission to the nursing school along with mundane things like exam results. And these lasses, for all their worthiness, were fractionally less likely to feature in the conversation of people like Jamie McTweed and his fellows, at such dens of conviviality as the White Rabbbit.

This hostelry was, by any civilized standards, a pretentious disaster of a place. Outside it was pseudo-Tudor, with black beams painted on to white stucco,and a white plastic wheelbarrow on the pavement planted with a few scruffy annuals which evidently did not take very seriously their duty to be ornamental. Inside it was even-more-pseudo Victorian with dark velvet curtains which were never pulled and a nicotine-tanned gloom which even garish plastic flowers failed to brighten. How it came to cower in the august shadow of so fine and worthy a building as St Lawrence's Hospital was something of a mystery. But there it was, just across the road, as bold as brass. Architectural anomaly, town-planning disaster or just plain eyesore, it was still more than redeemed in all but the most puritanical eyes by its proximity, a certain laxity of time-keeping to which the local police turned an obliging blind eye, and an unending supply of that nectar beloved of gods and medical men alike, draught Guinness. Even the most environmentally aware could be swayed by such virtues.

Over the years the White Rabbit had become little short of an unofficial annexe to the hospital. It could probably have kept going, if necessary, solely on the business brought in by hospital staff—off duty, semi off duty but officially on call, even, it must be admitted, officially *on* duty and 'called away urgently to another ward'. Every night was the same. At about the time the Larry's nurses, beautiful or not-so-beautiful, were doling out hot drinks, pills and potions, jabbing vicious needlefuls of antibiotics into complaining rumps and generally settling the wards in their tender care down for the night, the regulars of the White Rabbit were with equal dedication embarking on the evening's serious drinking. Medics, lab. workers, nurses, porters, even a patient or two. No barriers of rank or job. No questions asked; plenty of good company, some shop talk, a great deal of hospital gossip, oceans of draught Guinness. All just as a pub should be. So who really cared what the place *looked* like?

Jamie McTweed was a regular, needless to say, and was often to be found at this time of evening propping up the bar, the life and soul of the noisiest group of drinkers. But, not on this particular night. On this occasion he was quiet, preoccupied, definitely not his usual ebullient self as he stared balefully into the bottom of his tankard or glanced with unusual lack of interest at the provocative slip of lace which spelt the difference between triumph and disaster to the

12

neckline of the barmaid's dress.

In those days Jamie was still something of a medical student at heart, although his exams were a thing of the past and he was by now well settled into his first houseman's job. He no longer basked in being addressed as Doctor, nor walked with just the slightest swagger to show off the length of his white coat or wore his stethoscope continuously round his neck even when he did not need to use it, as if it was an Olympic gold medal. Indeed, while the realization was only slowly dawning on him that the very lowest form of life in the medical hierarchy of a big teaching hospital is not the most comfortable form of existence, the glamour of being a Real Doctor at last had certainly begun to wear a bit thin; and as his old healthy priorities reasserted themselves he realized, with some surprise and considerable relief, that the important things in life were still beer and girls with medicine running a rather poor third. And as far as the demands made upon him allowed, he took up the reins of existence which the tiresome intrusion of revision and exams had forced him to drop and return to cultivating and enjoying an exaggerated, but not entirely unfounded, reputation for being a Bit of a Lad.

His group of drinking friends, heaven help them, were no worse but certainly no better than he was, and the sort of conversation that ebbed and flowed noisily round him that evening was fairly predictable. What were the chances of one of their number, Charlie Wootton, making the hospital First rugger team this year? Generally dismissed as negligible because, *he* said, of pressure of b----- work. (No one questioned either the estimation of his chances or his choice of adjective.) What were anyone's chances of getting anywhere with that sexy-looking but cold-blooded sister who had taken over on Casualty and who was said to have done a course in karate, though whether to ensure the successful handling of St Lawrence's inevitable tide of Saturday-night drunks or in order to protect her reputation no one knew—or seemed particularly keen on finding out. Bob Scrivens, who had been sent packing firmly before he could so much as embark decisively on the chatting-up of negotiations, announced he preferred to get his kicks an easier way. There were universal groans.

'What do you suggest then?' somebody asked. 'Climb a six-foot wall, shin up a drain-pipe and risk your neck across that glass roof to play Peeping Tom outside the nurses' quarters?'

'No, that's old hat,' said Charlie Wootton. 'If you want a real thrill, I'm telling you, go and see that old war film at the flea pit. It's one of the ones with Susannah York as a Wren, and in one scene you actually see some of those old-fashioned suspenders and black stocking tops. Now that's the sort of thing that really turns a guy on.'

'It all depends on your taste,' said Peter Martin, an ophthalmics man who was mercilessly teased for wearing glasses himself. His voice was disdainful. 'Though the night I

saw the film I must admit the scene brought
forth a few ragged cheers from parts of the
auditorium.'

'Well, at least the rest of the film's good.
A bit more uplifting form of entertainment
than having us all put on dirty old macs and
queue in the rain to see that blue film in
Soho,' said Charlie. 'That was the last bright
idea anyone had for a day out, and a fine
bore it proved to be.'

'Go on,' maintained Monkey Smith, a tall
chinless wonder of a man involved in some
sort of anaesthetics course, whose nickname
came from his inordinately long arms and
his tendency to walk like a cross between an
ape and Groucho Marx. 'It was good for a
laugh.'

'So's a post-mortem by that standard.'

'And you're seriously suggesting it's worth
sitting through two hours of Lancaster
bombers, ops rooms and jolly old stiff upper
lips just for thirty erotic seconds of Miss
York's black elastic suspenders...?'

'Ah, nostalgia. I'm suggesting just that.

They simply don't make 'em like that any more.'

'Nuts! The girls are still the same underneath. Who cares about the wrapper when the toffee still tastes the same?'

'That's what I like about you, Monkey. You're so subtle! Why, nowadays there's no mystery to undressing a girl.'

'You're a doctor—I'm surprised there ever was any mystery for you.'

'It's all tights and roll-ons and special-shaped bras like they advertise on the telly—'

'Nonsense. With all this rot about women's lib half of them don't wear bras anyway...'

The discussion of such life-and-death issues was usually right up Jamie's street and he would normally be in there pitching with the best of them. Not tonight. Alas, his black moroseness continued unrelieved, unabated.

It was not just that he was exhausted. That was a generally accepted state of existence by that time of the day, as the whole bunch of them were finding out during these months of their first genuine encounter with hard work. They seldom escaped from the hospital for this spell in the evening in a condition anything short of what Monkey Smith referred to so elegantly as half-knackered.

No. It was something far more earth-shaking than that.

Hunched disconsolately on his bar stool, glaring at the bottom of his dry tankard, our friend was coming reluctantly face-to-face with one of the blindingly obvious, but un-doubtedly knottier, realities of life: that the main problem about being flat stony broke is that one simply does not have any money. None at all. Not even—perish the thought—for a pint of bitter to help one face the prospect.

He was disarmingly frank with them when his round came.

'I'm skint, boys,' he said.

There was a not-very-charitable silence.

'What, you?' scoffed Monkey Smith. 'Go on! Son of the great Sir John McTweed,

18

famous surgeon, author of all those standard textbooks—'

'One, actually.'

'Yes, but four volumes, dear boy, four volumes. Known and quoted in every plastic-surgery theatre in the land—'

'Come off it, Monkey. A man can't choose his parents. And what's the book got to do with it anyway?'

'Well, the great Sir John's stinking rich. Everyone knows that. How can you be broke?'

'Quite easily, I assure you. The old man's not badly off, you're right. But you needn't think I get a sniff of it till he kicks the bucket. Not even an allowance now that I'm earning. He's one of the "Let the boy stand on his own two feet like I had to" school. If I had a pound for every time I'd heard the bit about him being a self-made man I wouldn't be in a hole now.'

'Very touching,' agreed Bob Scrivens. 'Very touching indeed. But that doesn't make you any worse off than the rest of us

19

who have to stand on our own two feet and earn a living—just equal. And I, for one, am thirsty.'

He flourished an empty tankard under Jamie's nose.

'I'm broke in a good cause,' parried Jamie.

'Oh, yes. What cause?'

'A good one, believe me.'

'We don't.'

So much for the comradeship of drinking companions. The was nothing for it. Perhaps attack was the best method of defence.

Where were you at four o'clock this afternoon?' he fired in his best melodramatic CID style at the nearest of the circle, Pete Martin, who, taken by surprise, stammered back: 'I...haven't the least idea...four o'clock? On the ward, I suppose...Why?'

'Because at exactly that hour,' Jamie was enjoying making the most of his tale of woe, 'or perhaps a few disastrous minutes later to be precise, the most wonderful horse, an absolute paragon of horseflesh, supposedly the greatest thing since Blue what-was-his-name? the one with wings?'

'Bucephalus.'

'Thank you.'

'Not at all.'

'...with a pedigree like Burke's Peerage and form like an angel, which according to all the papers and predictions was absolutely bound to come sailing home in the last race at Ascot—'

'Didn't.'

'Not just didn't, it ran the sort of race that some spavined, three-legged nag of a milk-man's horse would have been ashamed of and came in seventh out of a field of ten.'

'Carrying your shirt with it, naturally.'

'That's the long and the short of it. A genuine stroke of misfortune that could happen to anyone.'

Confession was good for the soul and Jamie was feeling better already. He looked round the group. They were good chaps. There would be a general air of understanding, fellow-feeling and sympathy; who could tell, perhaps even a quick whip-round for a fellow who was down on his luck.

Not a bit of it.

'Well, *I'm* still thirsty,' said Bob Scrivens pointedly.

There was a murmur of agreement. Then, far from showing any form of sympathy, the pompous self-righteous wretches, as if they enjoyed kicking a man when he was down, stood round in a semi-circle so that he was pinned against the bar, empty beer mugs carefully in evidence, and took it upon themselves to lecture their unfortunate victim on the evil of his ways. Just as smug as you please—for all the world as if none of them had ever enjoyed a flutter in their lives. It was enough to make you sick.

'OK, fellows, OK,' our hero conceded with typical good humour. 'So I have a bit of a gamble once in a while. There's no harm in that.'

'There is, the way you do it.'

'I've never heard you complain when I win.'

'Ha! And how often is that, pray?'

'Nobody can win all the time.'

'You never do,' asserted Pete.

'Et tu, Brute?' said Jamie pathetically. 'Then die, Caesar.'

The classical allusion fell on stony ground.

'I never knew,' lectured Bob relentlessly, 'I never even imagined, that there could be so many blind, deaf, diseased and generally moribund horses disporting themselves on the racecourses of this country until I watched you picking out a few of your supposed dead-cert sure-fire winners.'

'All right. You've made your point. And you've all become mighty self-righteous all of a sudden, I must say. I can't see what business it is of yours anyway.'

'You bet your life it's our business when it's supposed to be your round and we're all standing here with empty glasses because you've thrown your money away on a horse.'

'Well, come on then. You're supposed to be my mates, aren't you? One of you lend me a few quid to be going on with till the end of the month.'

This perfectly reasonable suggestion was met with a spontaneous outburst of silence from the group.

Charlie Montague, an orthopod and a man of few words whose chief claim to fame was the possession of an apparently unslakeable thirst and a head like a rock to match it, shook his tankard mournfully and let the last drop or two fall on to the stained and threadbare carpet of the bar.

'Even just a half to be going on with,' he muttered to no one in particular.

'*You* lend him some money, then?'

'*Me?*' The genuine horror in his voice brought laughter which slightly relieved a situation where even the thick-skinned Jamie was beginning to feel a mite uncomfortable.

'Look,' Jamie began in a conciliatory tone, 'it's not my fault if...'

They were not listening. Heads close, they were conferring in a little group not unlike one of Charlie Wootton's scrums, or perhaps, thought Jamie, listening to the occasional adolescent splutters of mirth, more like a group of schoolgirls at half-time during a hockey match. The whispering ended in a short burst of conspiratorial laughter and the heads came up and turned towards him once more.

'Now gambling's not your only vice,' began Bob Scrivens sternly.

'Oh God, not another lecture!' objected Jamie. 'I'm going.'

'No, you're not. You're staying right where you are till you hear what we've got to say. You fancy yourself with the girls as well, don't you? Quite the modern Casanova, or so you'd have us believe.'

'You're a fine one to talk!'

That is neither here nor there. No, sit still and listen because we are going to do you a favour. You lost your money gambling and we're going to give you a chance to win it back—on a girl this time.'

'On a girl? What on earth do you mean?'

'I mean that I'll bet you...let's see, say thirty quid...yes, I'll bet you thirty quid that you can't seduce...who shall we say, fellows?'

'The plainest nurse in the hospital, whoever that is,' someone prompted.

'It must be Mousie Miniver.' This met
with fairly general agreement.

'All right. I'll bet that you can't seduce
Mousie Miniver—'

'That's not the sort of thing to bet about,'
objected Jamie.

'Oh my,' mocked Monkey Smith. 'The
man's got scruples. Or is it just because she
isn't a horse?'

'No, of course not, you dope. It's just
that...well, I don't know her, but I've seen
her around. She's not that sort of girl.'

'There wouldn't be much point in the bet
if she was.'

'Anyway,' maintained Bob. 'They're all
that kind of girl, given half a chance. Sisters
underneath the skin, and all that nonsense.
It'll make a bit of a change from your usual
type, the Selinas of this world.'

'There is no need to bring her into
it.'

Selina was a dark-haired, long-legged pussy cat of a girl, sleek nubile and very much Jamie's type; she parked her denim shoulder-bag at one of the secretary's desks in Miss Gray, the Principal Nursing Officer's outer office, and apparently got through the day there without doing anything constructive whatever except a bit of filing (not letters, her long, well-manicured nails). She was as near to a steady girl-friend as it suited Jamie to get—though he had been known to get pretty near to *her* on occasions...

'You're never afraid of a challenge, are you?' They confronted him.

'Of course not,' he objected fiercely. 'It's just that...'

'He wants to back out,' needled Pete. 'Like he backed out of buying the drinks.'

'I didn't *back out*,' Jamie was getting angry now, 'and I'm not trying to back out of this.'

'Oh, don't worry, we shall quite understand. We all know how easy it is to talk big and then have somebody call your bluff.'

'I am *not* trying to back out of anything!'

'Then you'll take the bet?'

In the silence all their eyes were on him, mocking and challenging.

There was no way out.

He was cornered. It was a pity they had picked quite such a plain girl, but they were right, she should not present any real problems once he put his mind to it, and what was one more scalp on his belt here or there anyway? And the thought of thirty quid was better than a dig with a blunt scalpel.

He shrugged, as nonchalantly as he could manage.

'Yes,' he said, 'I'll take it.'

'Good,' said Bob, holding out his hand. 'What about a drink on it?'

CHAPTER TWO

Nurse Carrie Masterson was eighteen, but she was feeling a lot younger than that as she faced her first spell of night duty on Women's Surgical. She was pretty new to nursing and had barely set foot on this ward for more than a couple of hours earlier in the day, supposedly to get her bearings. Her nerves had denied her even the few hours of sleep she might have snatched before the chilly nightmare occurred, that of having to get up and dress for work just when it was getting dark and the rest of the world was getting ready for sleep or looking forward to an evening's relaxation and entertainment.

The daytime staff nurse had sped cheerfully through the report in a sort of casual verbal shorthand which had obviously been sufficient for the senior on with her. But pieces of information like 'old Mrs Quiller had another of her turns today, we gave her the usual jab and she seems OK but you'd better keep an eye on her' were hardly calculated to allay the apprehensions of little Nurse Masterson. Which one was Mrs Quiller? What sort of turns were they? What sort of injections were they, what did they do? What happened if she wasn't given them? What were they keeping an eye on her for, what was she likely to do? What if she was with Mrs Quiller and she had another turn and she didn't know what to do...or if her senior had gone off to her meal and she was alone and supposed to be in charge of the ward and someone fell out of bed, or started haemorrhaging...or...or...a hundred terrifying possibilities rushed through her mind, all with one thing in common—she knew she would not have the first idea how to cope.

'Nurse, I still haven't had a bedpan.'
'Nurse, my pillows are all sliding down.'

'Nurse, this pain's getting worse. I asked the day staff for something but they must have forgotten.'

'Nurse, you've given me too much sugar in this cocoa. I only like a little. The other nurse who's usually on, she always gets it just right.'

'Yes, I'm sorry...I'm coming...I'll do it in a minute...I'm sorry...Yes, I'll ask the staff nurse...'

Oh, this was terrible, she would never get straight. How on earth did anyone get through all these different jobs and keep all these horrible, demanding patients happy?

She didn't even know who more than one or two of them were or what was wrong with them or their treatment or *anything*. And night sister would come round soon and expect her to know everything about them all and their conditions and when their operations were, even if it was her first night on and she was only a first year, or so the other girls had told her. Which were the post-operative patients anyway, and how could you tell? Were they the ones with the blue night-lights over their beds? Or the ones with drips up? What happened if one of the drips stopped? Or ran through? Or...Or...something.

During the daytime there were always so many nurses on a ward, all senior to her, there for her to turn to, efficient, cool, able to cope—all the things she so consciously, painfully was not. And now there was just her and the staff nurse, and she was not very sure of all the things she was meant to be doing, and she wished she was almost anywhere but here, and in a moment she was probably going to burst into tears and make an even worse idiot of herself...and...

'Yes, I'll take your bedpan away in a minute. I'm sorry. I haven't forgotten.

Where was that handkerchief of hers? Oh dear, this was even worse than she had expected...and there was that wretched old woman in the cubicle who needed her dentures cleaned and the woman with the flowers left from visiting which still had not been put into water and she couldn't find any vases so they were stuck in the sink in the sluice and—

'Nurse, can't you take this bedpan away? I've been here for hours.'

'I'm coming.'

'Nurse—'

'Nurse—'

'Oh, I'm coming, I'm coming. Please be patient, all of you!'

'Well, now, how are you getting on?' The cool voice slipped things quietly back into their proper perspective again. 'It's always a bit chaotic, your first night on. Don't worry, we've all been through it. *All right, dear, we'll be there in a minute.* Now I've finished the medicines and the temps, so we'll get the rest of these odd jobs finished together. Are all the hot-drink cups cleared away?'

'I think so.'

'Good. They're a real liability on lockers during the night, knock one of them flying and you wake everyone up. Now, you finish the last of the bedpans. Give me a call if there's anyone heavy and you need help getting them on or off—*all right, dear, we're on our way*—and I'll do the rest of the odd jobs around and start getting them settled down for bye-byes because we're a bit late tonight. We'll get the main lights out as soon as we can, so just have a quick look in the drawer of that big table and check that the torch is there; it's hopeless fumbling round looking for that in the darkness. We'll settle the major post-op cases together and I'll tell you a bit about them at the same time. There are only one or two of them tonight so with any luck we might be fairly quiet. Then you can put the kettle on and show off how good you are at making coffee and we'll have a well-earned sit down and run through the report again together down by the nursing station.'

'Right, Staff.'

'And try and cheer up, lovie. I know your first night on's not much fun, but you're not getting on badly at all, and I'm here to see you get through it all right. OK?'

'OK.'

'So treat yourself to a smile every so often, and cheer the patients up as well.'

'OK, Staff.' Perhaps things weren't going to be quite so unbearable after all.

It was the next morning.

'I'm telling you, she's a lovely girl, that Staff Nurse Miniver,' a middle-aged lady with a blue nightie with roses on it was chirping brightly, like first soprano sparrow in the ward's dawn chorus.

Comfortably installed in a corner bed and surveying the length of the ward as if she had been put there as some sort of benevolent supervisor, she was holding forth to everyone in general, and particularly to new arrival Mrs Janet Dunbar. 'She's the one with the blue belt and the pretty silver buckle, who's just given you your injection. I'll bet you hardly felt it, did you? No. There you are, you see. A lovely girl, ever such a good nurse, too. Won't hurt you if she can help it, and if something's going to be sore she tells you so. Now that's as it should be, I think, don't you? Because some of the things they do to you are bound to hurt, aren't they? We know that. I can tell you a thing or two about pain, believe me. I've been in and out of a few hospitals in my time, and when I say that Nurse Miniver's one of the best, I know what I'm talking about.'

Janet Dunbar was in no situation, or mood, to doubt her. And since nobody else down that end of the ward seemed inclined to disagree with her, or was even sufficiently wide awake, or spirited enough, to interrupt her, she went on: 'I've been in here ten days this time. Gall-bladder trouble. Cholecys-tightness the doctors call it, and oh, the pain was something terrible when they first brought me in. It started right in the middle of eating this trifle. We'd gone out to dinner because it was our wedding anniversary, you see, twenty-two years we'd been married. And we had this dinner, oh a lovely dinner it was, and then right in the middle…they were very good, mind, ever so kind and that, looked after me till the ambulance came…But that staff nurse, oh she was lovely. Nothing was too much trouble. Do you know, she even rinsed out my nighties for me because she knew there was only my husband at home; used to wash them out and hang them on the little radiator in the clinical room, she told me; even took them back to the nurses' home to iron once or twice and they're not supposed to do that…

'There aren't many would go to that trouble, mind. Some of them are proper flightly little madams, thinking of nothing but boy-friends and new clothes and getting off duty early. I suppose that's how it should be at that age. They're not too bad mostly, though, you'll see. Mind, now when my sister was in here last year, no I'm lying it must have been the year before…'

There was an empty bed between the talker and Janet Dunbar, and across the wide floor of the ward, under the row of windows on the opposite side, the first two beds were occupied by a well-sedated post-operative patient complete with drip running, bed-cradle in position and some weird and wonderful pump chugging away slowly and rhythmically at the head of the bed, and a teenager who turned out to be in hospital for a minor dental operation and whose only interest seemed to be the radio earphones and the full-colour, pull-out, pop-up, three-dimensional centrepiece of a magazine called *Gorgeous* which featured some lanky and miserably-undernourished specimen of hirsute manhood in leopardskin Y-fronts.

The complete lack of any sort of interested audience was no deterrent to the compulsive talker in the blue nightie, and even doped as she was Janet Dunbar was beginning to wish someone had slipped something into the woman's morning tea.

'Now when my husband was in here, well not actually in *here* because this is a woman's ward of course, but in this hospital—I can tell you the name of the ward if I think about it, a funny name it was, reminded me of a flower. There, it's gone. Have you ever noticed how you can remember some names quite easily until someone actually asks you, then you can't think of them to save your life. Anyway, he was in here, my Bert, having his hernia done—had to wait so long for a bed it was ten times worse by the time they did get round to having him in—anyway, the staff nurse on that ward was a proper little minx. Pretty little thing, mind, but she had to have everything just so, and my goodness the way she talked to some of those men! Old enough to be her father a lot of them and she had them cowering like little boys who hadn't done their sums right. Mind you, now, the sister on this ward's a pretty fair tartar at times—'

Through her haze Janet Dunbar heard footsteps coming down the ward as the nurse who seemed to be in charge came to make one of her regular checks on the postoperative patient. Janet watched, her eyes not really up to the effort of focusing

39

properly, as she put the stethoscope in her ears and pumped up the black cuff of the sphygmomanometer then let it down with a gentle hiss, took the patient's pulse and turned back the bedclothes briefly to look at a big abdominal dressing. She made some notes on the charts arrayed on the bedtable, watched the patient little pump ticking away industriously for a while, then counted the rate of the drips running through the infusion against the second hand on her watch and fiddled with the adjusting mechanism.

Encouraged now by the presence of a more promising audience, the blue nightie swept on with vigour: 'I was just saying, Staff, that the sister in charge of this ward, the one who's off duty now, is a right old cow.'

'Mrs Yardley, you should be ashamed of yourself. You know better than to talk like that, and you know very well you've no reason to complain about Sister Blandish.'

'Not personally, no—'

'Sister Blandish is a good nurse and a very

competent ward sister, you can take my word for it.' It was difficult to put much conviction into the words, but professional loyalty was dinned into them all through training and came naturally after so long.

'That's as maybe. I'm just saying she's an old ratbag. Deny that if you can—'

'Mrs Yardley, *please.*'

'You see, Staff, even you're trying not to laugh. She *is* and you know it.'

'You must not talk like that. What on earth are people going to think? We've a young patient here. And a new patient— whatever's she going to think?'

'The truth, that Sister's an old ratbag. And it won't take them five minutes to find that out for themselves anyway, so what's the harm in warning them.'

'Now, come on, Mrs Yardley. You know she's fairly reasonable as far as patients go—'

'Yes, but the way she treats you nurses! I tell you straight, I wouldn't stand for it.'

'Well, never you mind; nurses are a pretty resilient lot, you know. We've got skins like rhinoceroses and it takes more than the odd telling off from Sister to upset us. What you need to worry about is getting yourself well and out of hospital, or we'll all be telling you off.'

The footsteps came over to Janet Dunbar's bed.

'How are you feeling this morning?' the same voice asked. It was a quiet, friendly voice, and sounded as if it actually wanted to know.

Janet tried to open her eyes again, but it was difficult for more than a few seconds. Everything seemed a long way away and distinctly swimmy and she could not focus properly on anything without feeling a bit sick.

'This sounds silly but I don't really know,' she said. 'Rather giddy, I know that much.'

'That'll be the pethidine, I expect. It has that effect on some people. What about the pain?'

'That's better, much better. It's there still, but somehow I don't seem to worry about it any more. Does that sound nonsense to you?'

'No, I don't think so. In a few minutes it won't even be there. Now what I want you to do is to drink and drink as much as you possibly can. Breakfast will be here soon and you can eat if you want to—' Janet made a face—'though I don't expect you're very hungry, are you? But you must have at least one cup of tea, more if you can face it, and plenty of water or squash in between.'

'I'll try. But why?'

'The doctors aren't sure yet what is wrong with you, but one thing they suspect is a renal calculus, which sounds complicated but is quite simply a stone in the kidney, and sometimes if you drink enough fluid you can flush it out. And because they want to know if you do manage to get rid of it that way, you must ask for a bedpan each time and not go to the toilet, even if you feel up to it, OK?'

Janet nodded sleepily. The pain was

almost gone now, and the sense of nothing-
ness in its place was a luxury that she didn't
want to spoil even with the effort of words.

'Are you warm enough?' A hand felt her
forehead, then her cheek. She has gentle
hands that staff nurse, thought Janet, not big
clumsy hands like the porters who had
bundled her and her trolley up the corridor
from Casualty to X-ray and then, it seemed
hours later, along to the big lifts and up to
the ward; who would have thought there
were so many corners for a trolley to bump
into? Or that a lift door could be jolted shut
with such apparent venom? They were car-
ing, considerate hands, not like the girl in
X-ray who had pushed her and pummelled
her into the positions required for the
photographs as if she was some vast mound
of dough to be kneaded or an obstinate lump
of clay confronting a determined artist. A
simple request might easily have achieved
the same result—she was not moribund or
stupid, or even unco-operative, after all.

'There now, are you comfortable?' Staff

nurse's gentle hands eased the bedclothes a bit higher round her shoulders. What did the old bore in the blue nightie say her name was? Miniver or something. Wasn't there a book or a play or something about someone with a name like that? She must try to remember when she wasn't feeling so dopey.

'Oh, I nearly forgot to tell you, your husband rang a few minutes ago.' Janet knew this was important and tried to force herself to concentrate. 'He just wanted to know how you were, and said to give you his love and tell you the boys were being good and they're all managing a treat so you're not to fret, and they hope to be in to see you later. Now if you need us or the pain gets bad again, the buzzer is just here. It's on a sort of flex and I've put it right on the edge of your locker so that you can reach it easily.' One of the gentle hands just touched her hair in a gesture of reassurance and encouragement. Then the voice added very softly, 'And if Mrs Yardley and her chattering gets on your nerves, you tip us the wink, OK?'

Janet tried to say something but heard her voice come out as a sort of grunt. The footsteps went away, the background noises of the ward became more and more blurred, and gratefully she sank into a sort of in-between world, not asleep, not aware of what was happening round her either. Conscious inside her mind, grateful for the absence of pain and half afraid all the time that it might return.

Was it really only yesterday morning, twenty-four hours ago, that she had woken up at home as she always did, nudged Angus awake, made them both a cup of tea, called to the boys to wake up, and set out to face another apparently normal run-of-the-mill day? She did not want to get up, she remembered. There was nothing unusual in that, she seldom did. Her first suspicion that all was not well was a distinct twinge of pain while she was cooking the breakfast, not one of the familiar aches and pains, old friends, indigenous to each person, but a strange pain, sharp, insistent and searing. It passed off, and she almost forgot it, getting Angus packed off to work and the boys bullied into their blazers and caps and off to school with the usual demonstrations of affection and cheerfulness.

Then, left alone, she cleared the table automatically, filled the washing-machine with the weekend's dirty clothes and set it to work, then made herself her customary cup of coffee before facing the sinkful of dirty dishes and saucepans from supper the night before.

It was no use pretending. That pain was there again. She winced mentally just remembering it. As if someone had driven a sword with a thin, red-hot blade right into her side somewhere at about waist level, and then explored inside her with the point, twisting and turning.

It was probably wind, she told herself. Everybody knew what agony that could be. Some of that white peppermint mixture, a strong cup of coffee, then some exercise, like changing the beds, for instance, that was all she needed...wasn't it? An expert at reassuring, like every mother, she wished she was as easily convinced by her own optimism this time.

The pain eased a little—there, of course it was only wind all the time—then came back an hour or so later rather worse. Did she feel sick, or was it the very fact of the pain that was having that effect in the same way as a bad enough pain anywhere else would? She could not tell but she was longing for some friendly sympathy from someone without actually admitting to herself that she needed a doctor.

Half-way through the morning Margaret Llewellyn rang. She wanted to talk about the meeting to discuss the fete to raise money for spastics, or pit ponies, or guide dogs, or handicapped racehorses or something; she had so many pet charities Janet could never keep count—she just knew *she* had been bulldozed into letting her house be used for the meeting. Margaret was one of those overwhelming ladies who knew everything and everybody and not only had a solution for every possible problem but managed to cram both it and its obviousness down the throat of the poor person concerned until they felt totally inadequate and somewhat put upon. She was also a full-time committee lady with a knack of bullying half-willing helpers into doing about three times more than they originally bargained for and leaving them markedly short of credit for their good deeds at the end of it.

'Good old Margaret, she's done it again,' people would say. 'She can get anyone to do anything for her, I don't know how she manages it.' Those who knew her powers of persuasion just kept quiet, and steered well clear of her on similar future occasions.

When Margaret rang to check the time and date of the meeting and confirm that Janet had indeed agreed to provide a light buffet lunch afterwards (had she really? wondered Janet), the pain was at its worst and she was near to tears. She was tempted to confide in her friend, but Good Old

Margaret, with all her love for man and animal kind in the abstract, never seemed to have very much time for actual people with actual pains. She would probably reel off a dozen sure-fire cures tried and tested for *far* worse pains by various family and friends, cures that probably relied largely on griting the teeth, grinning and bearing it and demonstrating the power of mind over matter. Janet decided to waive the dubious possibility of receiving sympathy and kept quiet.

All day the pain grew worse. Her complete lack of appetite at lunchtime worried her, too. With a constant weight problem, lack of appetite was one thing she seldom experienced. By mid-afternoon things were really getting out of hand. Short, comparatively free periods, when she tried desperately to pretend that all was well, were interrupted by great tidal waves of pain, which had her rolling around on the floor, bent up double, crying out in her misery, and leaving her weak, scared and totally demoralized.

During one of the intervals between the worst of the attacks she managed to get off the sofa and across to the telephone on the semi-circular table at the other side of the sitting-room.

Now, what was that wretched doctor's number? She ought to know it well enough, she needed it often enough when the boys were ill. She knew well enough what to expect when she got through. The receptionist, like some well-trained dragon whose mission in life was to keep doctor and patient apart, would argue and bitch and question everything she said. Was a visit really necessary? If so, why hadn't she phoned earlier in the day, before Doctor (her voice implied the capital letter. Why couldn't she call him *the* doctor?) went out on His rounds? You didn't need a visit *then?* Oh, so this must have been sudden then' (the tone of voice all but implied trumped up). And at last the reluctant: 'Oh, well, I suppose you'd better give me the details.'

In fact today was mercifully different. Perhaps her voice betrayed her desperation. The receptionist was not obstructive, seemed almost helpful in fact, and would get Doctor to come round as soon as she could reach him.

Surprised and immensely relieved, Janet slumped back on to her sofa and immediately—now that help was on its way—began to feel better and even to think the pain had gone away altogether and had perhaps been no more than her imagination. Not for long though. Next time the red-hot sword went into action the pain did not even bother to lurk quietly in the background gathering strength. It was all there suddenly, demanding her full attention, blotting out the thought of anything else, making her cold, yet sweating, almost sick with the sheer intensity of it. And with fear—what *was* it, for Gods sake?

When the doctor arrived, smelling of medicated soap and reassurance, she somehow got herself to the front door to let him in. Automatically, she mumbled apologies for the state of the house.

He did all the usual listenings and proddings and probings.

Did it hurt when he pressed here with his hands? Was it tender there? Or there?

No. Yes. To be honest, she wasn't sure (raised eyebrow). The coolness of his hands seemed in itself a sort of salve to the pain, and it was difficult to tell where it really was.

He grunted tolerantly. Had she been sick? Had she been to the toilet normally? When was her last period? And a dozen more questions, with each response greeted by a noncommittal grunt.

At last he straightened up.

'Well, I think it should be hospital for you, my dear. Where's your telephone, and I will get it fixed up. But I'm sorry I can't give you anything for the pain, or I might go masking symptoms that are important in finding out what's causing it.'

She did not know how long it was until the ambulance came, or which way the driver took through the Titchford streets. She remembered trying to phone Angus while she waited, being told he was at an important meeting, leaving a message with that nice little secretary of his, who was all sympathy and offers of help. Then that dreadful bumpy ride, each motion of the great heavy vehicle jarring until she wanted to scream. Reassuring voices, but brusque hands, hands of people who meant well but were not themselves in pain and could not understand; the chilly wait in Casualty until the houseman came.

'Hallo,' he said, I'm Dr Doyle.' How young he looked, not much older than the boys. Wasn't it supposed to be a sign you were getting old when doctors started looking young? Or was it policemen? She could not remember. He seemed to have plenty of self-confidence anyway, and the nurses, who seemed even younger, treated him with respect.

More probings and proddings. More questions, mostly the same ones. Long waits.

'I'm sorry, dear, nothing for the pain yet...'
A rough trundle down the corridor to X-ray, where Angus caught up with her, having managed to cut short his meeting. He sat by the trolley, holding her hand, still in his smart shirt and tie and best suit, but no longer the manager, the business executive, suddenly in need of comfort and reassurance just as much as she was. They hardly spoke. There was not much to say once she had described her nightmare day and he had told her the arrangements he had made for the boys until he could get home. He just sat, grinning nervously and squeezing her fingers from time to time.

He would bring her things in next day.

He would remember that there were clean underpants and socks for the boys in the airing cupboard.

And that his jacket should be ready for collection from the cleaners.

And that neither of them would eat eggs for breakfast.

'Hold your breath now.' Whirr, click.

'That's good.'

'Can I move? It's hurting.'

'Not yet, dear, I want another shot like that.' Whirr, click.

'Now I want you like this.'

'Ouch.'

Whirr, click. On and on. Had Angus come to the ward, or gone home to get the boys to bed earlier? She couldn't remember. Only the hands, the pushing and the hurting, the bumpy trolley. Then the cool, crisp sheets of the ward bed, complete exhaustion, and at last the staff nurse with a syringe, and the blessed relief of pethidine...and sleep.

CHAPTER THREE

The first step in Jamie McTweed's plan of campaign was obvious. He would have to strike up some sort of acquaintance with this Miniver kid. The prospect frankly bored him, but at least there was the element of challenge, and of cash at the end of the campaign, to stir the adrenalin. He knew her vaguely by sight of course, as one knew a hundred people who had been around the hospital in different capacities during the same years as one had oneself. But unless you worked on the same ward or department or your paths crossed socially, there it usually stopped. You were surrounded, like regular commuters on London trains, by dozens of people you knew but did not know.

Anyway the sooner he got to know Mousie

Miniver, and pretty closely at that, the better. Pondering this step occupied at least a part of his mind during his ward round next morning, as he trundled the heavy trolley of notes round Men's Medical (surely the average trolley of medical notes weighed more than its equivalent of notes for surgical patients, he thought, as he did every time he pushed it out—they ought to put motors on them, or at least seats and handlebars like hot-dog sellers), enquiring tenderly after the state of health of each of his charges, and trying to show suitable interest in the lengthy answers. So often these degenerated into grumbles. One old chap wanted to know why his treatment was taking so long. He had been told he could go home within a fortnight and *that* was more than three weeks ago. Tell him as tactfully as possible that if he would only remember to do the necessary into a bedpan each time so that the nurses could secure the set of specimens the path. lab. needed, instead of determinedly using the loo in spite of reminders, beggings, and pleadings, everyone might be able to get on a bit quicker.

Another objected strongly because every time the Draculas from the lab. came round for blood he was on their list. Tell him there must be a mistake and you will look into it. Fob him off somehow. Far be it from *you* to divulge that the registrar is doing a blood-group study, and he has the misfortune to be the only D-negative available, so there he had to stay wasting his time and blocking a bed until the study is finished. A houseman did not query such things, just kept his mouth shut and fielded the difficult questions as best he could.

Old doddery Jock in the next bed was a cheerful old chappie who caused some amusement by trying to light up his pipe under the bedclothes when he thought Sister wasn't around. He was apparently unaware that the smell permeated the whole ward in a matter of seconds, and he was always indignant, believing that someone must have betrayed his secret. He wanted to know why his painful varicose ulcers should take so long to heal. Lecture him—gently, mind, he's a nice old fellow, but still lecture him, your white coat carries a lot of authority— on the importance of leaving the dressing alone. Nothing will heal if the dressing is yanked aside with grubby fingers several times a day; it is worse than digging up a seed to see if it is growing. The old chap liked that and grinned. He was a farm worker, and that made sense to him.

One young man actually felt better, but he seemed to be in a gallant minority, and Jamie felt depressed, as he usually did on Men's Medical. More grumbles. How should *he* know why the food was always cold by the time it reached them? How was *he* supposed to stop the night nurses sounding as if they had stormtroopers' boots on and dropping bedpans in the sluice in the small hours of the morning. They seemed to think he was some sort of ward ombudsman, while he sometimes felt that his lowly voice carried less weight than their own on almost any subject.

Into the office with a sigh of relief. He checked through the returned path. slips before filing them. Nothing revolutionary there. Somewhere in the white coat pocket was a list of further tests and work-ups demanded on the poor suffering victims in there. And he'd better dream up one or two of his own as well. It kept the backroom boys in a job, kept the nursing staff on their toes and helped to impress the boss if and when he elected to do a round (not today mercifully. Today was his day for playing golf with the chairman of the board of governors, and heaven help the hapless patient in an emergency and the unfortunate junior doctor whose summons interrupted that hallowed appointment.)

He made a few perfunctory additions to the notes, nothing earth-shaking, just entries under today's date as a way of registering the fact that he had duly been on station and doing his job as required. Then, as ever in search of diversion from the unpleasant

day-to-day realities of other people's illnesses, he wandered into the clinical room,
where staff nurse Mackie, renowned for the
trimmest pair of ankles in the hospital, was
(eternally, it seemed) tidying something or
other and busily laying up a trolley. Funny
creatures, nurses. They say when a cat is in
doubt it washes itself. When a nurse is in
doubt, or, as he suspected, can't think of any
better way of appearing fully occupied, she
goes and lays up a trolley for something or
other. Well, so long as it was not some procedure he was meant to be doing and had
forgotten, or not been warned, about...

'Hallo, gorgeous.' He had a hand on her
waist before she heard him coming.

'Oh, *you.*' She pushed him unceremon-
iously away. 'Look what you've made me do
now. I shall have to start counting all over
again.'

'Have I ever told you how sexy you look
when you're trying to concentrate?'

'Yes,' she said, 'twenty-six, twenty-seven,
twenty-eight...'

'And your ankles are a work of art?'

'Yes,' she said, 'frequently. Thirty-nine, forty.'

Never mind, today he had more important business in hand than making progress with her, however commendable she might prove as a longer-term project.

'By the way,' he said casually, 'that staff nurse on Women's Surgical. Quiet little thing, Miniver or something like that I think her name is. Do you know her?'

'Hands off,' she said, without looking up from the box of disposable needles she was checking.

'Sorry?'

'Yes,' she said. 'I know her quite well. Hands off. She's not your type.'

'Who said anything...?' he began, then changed his mind. 'You in charge this morning?'

'That's right. You can always tell from the air of well-organized apathy.'

'Well, if I'm needed. I've gone down to the canteen for a quick coffee.'

'Strong and black for a hangover, as usual?'

'I shall treat that remark with silent contempt, as it deserves. Be a sweet girl and lend me a quid, would you? I was in a rush this morning and must have left my money on the dressing table.'

'If you've got half an hour for a coffee, I'm surprised you haven't time to go and get it. Still, just this once, because I've got a kind heart—'

She fetched her sling shoulder-bag from the nurses' changing room and gave him the money.

'You're a good girl, Mackie,' he said. 'I'll remember you in my will. You see if I don't.'

'You'd better remember me a darned sight sooner than that,' she said coldly. 'You're not the only one who's broke.'

The canteen was surprisingly crowded. Nurses with early coffee breaks from the wards jostled with members of housekeeping teams and the occasional office worker.

A group of lab. technicians and one or two brown-coated porters were smoking at the few tables in the corner nearest the window where smoking was permitted, and there were one or two junior medics like himself among the last of the night nurses and the lie-abeds with days or long mornings off duty. It was all very democratic in here nowadays, even if it did not have quite the atmosphere of the White Rabbit.

Luck was with him that morning. There, nearly at the end of the queue for the counter, was Mousie Miniver. He grabbed himself a nasty brown wooden tray, shook the last drips of the previous user's coffee off it, and joined the line a couple of places behind her. The two intervening nurses were waiting for something cooked to materialize from behind the scenes, and Jamie managed to slide quietly past them, then take his place behind Mousie M, pretending to slow down in order to assess the relative merits of the various lumps of stale cake in the glass case. As they came up to the cash desk there was a hold up of some five or six people, so the next bit was easy—a quick sideways step, a jab of the elbow at just the opportune moment, and hey presto! just as neat as you please. One clumsy houseman covered in confusion an full of apologies, and one unfortunate staff nurse with coffee sluicing all down the front of her clean white apron.

'Oh, I say, I'm most dreadfully sorry. That was frightfully careless of me. I don't know how it can have happened, except that there was so much jostling round that cash desk, what with people queuing up and trying to get knives and forks and so on. Here, do let me see if I can clean you up a bit with some of these paper napkins.'

'It's all right. Really. Please don't worry. I'm sure it wasn't your fault, and these accidents will happen, won't they?'

'Are you sure you're not hurt? I mean scalded or anything? Not that the coffee here's usually hot enough to scald anyone.'

She laughed shyly. 'No, really. I'm quite all right. It hasn't even soaked through my uniform dress.'

A bit more ineffectual dabbing and mopping, then what could be more natural than to offer to buy her another coffee, and drink it with her.

'Thank you, but there's no need.'

'Of course there is; it's the very least I can do after that.'

The queue, in the way that queues have, had now evaporated, and it took him only half a minute to buy fresh coffees and join her at a table for two near the window. They introduced themselves, rather stiltedly. Polite conversation was obviously the order of the day. It was hardly one of Jamie's A-level subjects, but having started off well he was not going to lose the initiative now.

'I hope that wasn't your last clean apron or anything like that.'

'Oh, no.'

'Good. I wouldn't want you getting into trouble because of me.' An unfortunate remark, perhaps. Certainly one for which most of the girls of Jamie's acquaintance would have had a saucy reply ready. How on earth did he manage to get himself landed with an innocent like this one, he wondered.

He learned quite a lot about her during that first meeting, mostly by prodding and prompting her to talk about herself, unwilling as she was, at least to begin with, as the simplest way of keeping some sort of conversation going. Her real name was Shirley. She probably never thought of it as being a particularly pretty name, but then, he thought, probably nobody had ever whispered it to her in just the right way. On the other hand she would quite obviously have been thoroughly miserable if she had realized how many of the medical staff and students at the hospital, how many of her working colleagues, from technicians to registrars, and even, because such things are infectious, how many of her patients too, referred to her behind her back as Mousie. Happily she quite evidently did not realize it.

The most charitable of her friends could

not have denied her ordinariness, he decided, watching her as she talked. She had long hair of a nondescript—a mousie—mid-brown which was scraped back from her face as firmly as if she wished she could hide it all under her staff nurse's white cap. She wore glasses (with rather unbecoming round frames) because she was short-sighted. She always had been, she said, ever since her schooldays when she was chided by teachers and teased by pupils for her slowness when really she was just scared to admit that she simply could not read the writing on the blackboard. When one particularly sympathetic teacher noticed that her mental arithmetic and other oral work was far better than her written efforts and sent her to have her eyes tested, it turned out that she was really rather bright. The chiding from teachers stopped, but since she was now condemned to the regulation children's spectacles with round wire frames and hooks that punished her ears, the teasing from other children merely altered its target. She accepted it in good part and soon all but the real bullies left her alone, but she came inevitably to think of the glasses partly as a necessary evil but also as a barrier and a protection, however fragile, between herself and the not-always-friendly outside world. Perhaps, subconsciously, she still did.

She wore very little make-up. The hospital authorities, through their chief spokesman on such matters, Sister Plackett, the tutor whose mission in life was to mother, hen-peck, and generally boss the bewildered batches of girls who made up each new nursing intake through their introductory course, went to some lengths to stress the importance of a neat appearance and how too much, or too bright, lipstick, heavy eye shadow, all forms of coloured nail varnish, any sort of perfume, jewellery and other than wedding rings or any other personal adornment, except in due course a staff nurse's silver buckle and the hospital badge, were absolutely forbidden on duty. For most of the girls this sort of lecture was water off a duck's back and when it came to the point they mostly got away with far more in both make-up and personal adornment of all sorts than should theoretically be countenanced. But Shirley listened and, seeing the reasoning behind the instructions, followed them to the letter. Unusual, thought Jamie, I suppose even rather admirable in an odd sort of way. But how dull, my God, how deadly dull.

A pleasant, harmless, easy-going sort, he decided. Going through life minding her own business; probably, since she was hardly pushy or ambitious or loud-voiced, sometimes ignored, overruled, taken advantage of; one of nature's willing horses who got all the work and not much of the praise. Mackie was right—not his type at all.

But for the poor kid to be saddled with a name like Mousie! Mousie Miniver! It really did seem a bit unkind.

'Do you like working nights?' he said.

'No, I don't think anyone does. But at least with internal rotation being introduced it'll mean that we work far shorter spells than in the old nightmare days. I've nearly finished this stretch anyway; I'll be back on days again soon.'

'That'll be an improvement, I expect.'

'Yes, in some ways.'

Jamie felt his sunny grin beginning to crack round the edges a bit, but he persevered, determined to get a foot firmly in the door on this first meeting.

'Only in some ways?'

'Working at night at least you're left to get on with your job. Day duty means seeing a whole lot more of Sister Blandish and that is very much of a mixed blessing. I can tell you.'

'I've heard of her, but not crossed swords with her. What's she like?'

'I think you, being a Scotsman, would use the word dour.'

'And you? What word would you use?'

'I don't know. Cow, I think. Something not very charitable, anyway. I had to tell one of the more talkative patients off this morning for referring to her as an old rat-bag, but it was all I could do not to start laughing. It really sums her up very well. She was in one of her stroppy moods this morning and went on and on over report. I've got a very green junior on at the moment and she was picking on her all the time over things she could not possibly be expected to know. That's why we were so late off duty. I suppose she's what you might call one of the old school of sisters. Still, at least she's fairly reasonable to the patients and keeps the rough edge of her tongue for staff. That's something—at least, I suppose it is.'

Mousie began to clear the cups and plates on to one of the trays.

Jamie racked his brains for something to say, just to keep the dying conversation on its feet.

'Bill Doyle's the houseman on there, isn't he? How does he make out with her?'

She laughed. 'Not at all if he can help it. She's got her beady eye on our Dr Doyle, I reckon. Really fancies him from all accounts, and he spends most of his time keeping as much distance between the two of them as he can.'

'And you? Do you fancy him?'

'Me? No. I mean, he's very nice but—'

'Not your...what's the word?...not your steady?'

'No,' she said. 'I haven't got a steady.'

There was a directness about her which he found frankly rather unnerving, probably because of the dissembling inherent in his own role in the relationship. But, unabashed, he looked across the table, straight into her eyes. (When you looked at them behind those dreadful headlamps they weren't such bad eyes. Not such bad eyes at all. Quite a pleasant dark shade of brown. They looked at you a bit too straight for comfort, though.)

'I'm surprised to hear that, Shirley,' he said, and was gratified to see an unmistakable blush infuse the round owlish face.

That's your Impression made, McTweed, he told himself. Definitely fifteen love. Now clear out before you have a chance to spoil everything.

As if by magic, before he had even figured out a good exit line, the bleep in his pocket sounded.

'Excuse me, won't you. No peace for the wicked, eh?'

And he beat a hasty retreat, leaving her gathering dirty coffee cups to her like a mother hen marshalling her brood.

As chatting up birds goes, it had been pretty heavy work. But he was in no doubt that he had won the first round, if only on points. He was satisfied enough with his morning's work.

He picked up the internal phone at the end of the corridor.

'McTweed here. You were bleeping me.'

'Just a moment, please.' That was all that girl ever seemed to say. Tell her her tights were on fire and she'd say, 'Just a moment, please.'

'Yes, Dr McTweed. Casualty want you. I'll put you through.'

He waited patiently, pleasantly distracted by a more-than-adequately filled-out blue uniform passing on the way to the canteen. There is something at the same time so chaste and yet so suggestive about the way the bib part of a nurse's starched apron creases over a full bustline—somehow at the same time permanently virginal and yet eminently accessible.

What was Miniver's bustline like? He must be slipping, to his shame he had not even noticed.

'Er...hallo, yes, I'm here.'

'Casuality staff nurse speaking. We've had advance radio warning from the ambulance crew. A man has collapsed in Beech Place Market, suspected coronary. They're bringing him in.'

'OK,' said Jamie. 'I'll be right down.'

CHAPTER FOUR

Janet Dunbar was not, as she recollected later, in a fit state to notice much of what went on round her on that first full day in hospital. At first she was still half dopey from the pethidine, content to lie still, half dozing, half watching the goings-on in the ward, not moving her position in the bed in case that should prompt the pain to return.

The newspaper man came round soon after breakfast. He had his magazines and papers neatly laid out on a stretcher trolley borrowed from Casualty, and he greeted all his customers with the same cheerful over-familarity.

'Morning, darling. How you doing today? *Sun* as usual, is it. 'You are my sunshine, my only—' Ta, love. Hallo, ducks, you don't

look so bright this morning, getting you
down are they? Never mind, here's your
magazine with the knitting patterns in it,
they'll take your mind off it, put a copy by
for you specially. Good Lord, expect me to
change a fiver, you must be joking, don't
know when I last saw a fiver in my line of
business. Never mind, hang on to it and pay
me tomorrow. Here you are, Mrs. *Daily
Mail* and *Titbits*, and you're lucky to get it,
too. That's my last copy. I was keeping it
for a chap on the other ward, but he's gone
home. There you are, love, must be your
lucky day.'

He stopped by Janet's bed.

'Paper, love?' He cast an expert eye over
the few belongings on her locker and bed
table. '*Telegraph*, I expect, is it?'

'Oh...er...yes. Thank you. How did you
know?'

'Student of 'uman nature, that's me, love.
Spot a *Telegraph* reader a mile away.'

Feeling slightly abashed, Janet hauled
herself cautiously up in bed, and fumbled

in her purse. The man was grinning at her.

'Don't worry, dearie, I'm not really psychiatric, you know. There's a copy of yesterday's *Telegraph* on your chair.'

Of course. Angus must have left it here after his visit last night. She vaguely remembered him saying something cheerful about how she might feel like doing the crossword later on.

She took today's copy, glanced at the headlines and put it, folded, on the locker to look at later in the day.

'Hallo, sweetheart.' He passed on to the bed where the teenager with the teeth was sitting dangling her legs over the side of the bed, earphones on, looking bored. 'No, sorry. No chewing-gum. No sweets at all. Got a smashing book here, though. Pull-out poster of the Bay City Rollers in the middle. There, how's that? Look all right on your locker that would. No? Oh well, please yourself.'

'Are you still here? How do you manage to take all morning over a simple paper round, I wonder? Be gone with you now, we have work to get through on this ward.' The speaker was a tall, thin, prunes-and prisms-faced woman in a dark blue uniform and lacy cap. She was standing at the foot of Janet's bed comparing a piece of paper attached to a clipboard in her hand with one of the boards of notes at the foot of the bed. It could only be Sister Blandish.

'Morning, darling.' The man treated her to just as much familiarity as the patients. 'Just on my way then. Till tomorrow, ladies.'

The blue figure tutted her tongue impatiently at his departing back, and turned her attention to Janet.

Marion Blandish was one of those phenomena which occur in the ranks of any profession, especially one where too many women work together, their frictions eased by too few male colleagues. She was a real live spinster-type bitch. There are far fewer of them around nowadays than there used to be, life being generally so much more free and easy and attitudes more broad-minded. But somehow, there she was, the tyrant of Women's Surgical. She had, though naturally she would never admit it, joined the nursing profession as much to get her man as from any of the more acceptable high-minded motives. She wanted to be a doctor's wife (sometimes, she felt, she just wanted to be anybody's wife...), settling down to kids and domesticity, a life of security with the strength of the Women's Institute around her.

As so it should have been. She was not bad-looking in a craggy sort of way, and quite pleasant, at least to begin with, particularly when she put herself out. And there were one or two close shaves in the early days, which for one reason or another did not work out, leaving her embittered but determinedly optimistic. She qualified and moved up the usual rungs of the nursing ladder, one of a decreasing group as first one then another of their original set got engaged, then married, or went off into the big wide world outside the hospital to seek their fortunes in other jobs. And as, gradually, she began to get desperate about her future, and visualize herself in nursing for good (no other career attracted her and at least she knew and was good at this job), she gave vent to her frustration in the most readily available way—the pecking order.

She also began to gain herself an unenviable reputation for setting her cap at any remotely eligible male (and a few pretty ineligible ones) who crossed her path. Anyone who wanted to raise a cheap laugh in the White Rabbit had only to suggest it was time Blandish was transferred to a men's ward... and anyone who wanted to gain a reputation for charity might try pointing out that she wasn't really such a bad old stick, not if you treated her properly, and after all, everyone has problems...

'You came in yesterday, did you?' were her first words to Janet Dunbar.

'Yes. Yesterday evening.'

'My day off.' The tone of voice was faintly accusing.

'Oh. I'm sorry.' She was obviously supposed to have borne this fact in mind when embarking on her not-to-be-forgotten day of pain.

'You're for IVP this afternoon, so you're not to eat or drink anything until you get back from X-ray.'

'But...'

'But what, Mrs Dunbar? Don't I make myself clear?'

'Oh...yes...it's just that I was told I was to drink as much as I possibly could to try and clear the stone, if it is one.'

'And *I*'m telling you not to eat or drink anything until after they have done the IVP. All right?'

'Yes.'

The thin blue figure moved off up the ward, pausing to tell off the lady with the varicose veins and the big crepe bandages for creases in the regulation green counterpane on her bed which could only, it seemed, have been made by someone lying on it, strictly against regulations.

'Don't say I didn't warn you,' crowed the gall bladder in the blue nightie with roses. 'It's going to be a right cheerful day for everybody now that she's back on duty.'

'She made it sound as if I'd *chosen* to come in on a day when she wasn't here,' said Janet, a bit shaken by the unpromising first encounter with this woman who would obviously have considerable authority over her existence in the immediate future.

'Oh yes, that's typical. Mind you, if you'd had any sense you *would* have chosen to.' The woman laughed at her own joke. Janet felt a little better. If everyone was victim to this brusque woman perhaps things were not so bad. As soon as you step inside the hospital door it's You and Them, she thought. Patients and hospital staff, the ruled and the rulers. However kind and friendly They are, They have an unquestionable authority, the sort of power that staff have over children at a boarding school; and when they are not so kind and friendly you feel uncomfortably vulnerable and at their mercy. Being in night clothes and in bed while they are not only dressed but dressed in uniform did not put you in any stronger a position psychologically either. Even the cheerful, chatty members of the housekeeping team in their green overalls seemed somehow to take on something of this omnipotence.

Janet found herself just about to ask for further enlightenment on this IVP ordeal that loomed like some unspecified torture on the day's hitherto calm horizon from, of all people, the kindly blousy redhead called Flo, who dusted lockers and refilled water jugs. She seemed the most approachable one of Them. Then Janet quickly pulled herself together. The fact that Flo was wearing some sort of a uniform in hospital did not automatically bestow medical knowledge on her.

Still, it would have been nice if someone could have been a bit more communicative...

Margaret Llewellyn had a Friends of the Hospital committee meeting at St Lawrence's that morning, and when she heard that her *dear* friend Janet Dunbar was ill and had been admitted to Women's Surgical of course she simply *had* to come along a few minutes early to look in and see her first. After all, she was not without a little influence with the hospital authorities, and if she did not feel her friend was being treated exactly the way she ought to be, a word from her, Mrs Margaret Carruthers Llewellyn, in the right ears would surely put everything to rights. The proper use of such power as one had in life was so *terribly* important after all, wasn't it?

Thus it was that a bunned and tweeded figure, having blandly appropriated one of the coveted Doctors Only parking spaces in the courtyard in front of the hospital for her estate-car full of small assorted yapping dogs, was to be seen sweeping along the hospital corridors that morning. She looked with warm approval at a large poster advertising the Friends of the Hospital's major fund-raising function of the year, Matron's Ball (the title long since out of date, but maintained by long tradition) in the organization of which she was, needless to say, a leading light; nearly skittled down that rather self-satisfied and far-too-long-haired young houseman she had aired disparaging views on at the last Friend's committee meeting (what was his name, McTweed or something) as he made towards Casualty, white coat flapping open untidily, at what seemed an unnecessarily undignified speed; eyed with distaste a plain-looking little staff nurse whose face seemed vaguely familiar but whose name was unknown to her and who appeared to have spilt an entire cup of coffee down her uniform and was trying to hide the fact as best she could as she headed for the nurses' home; and paused to glare at the paper man who had by now returned to the big concourse of corridors known among the hospital staff as Leicester Square to spread his remaining papers and magazines out along one of the seats (rumour had it that he had been selling cigarettes and tobacco in the men's wards. This was forbidden, of course, and if it had been allowed it should have been the sole prerogative of the Friends of the Hospital trolley).

And so, not long after the morning coffee came round the ward, reducing poor thirsty Janet Dunbar to an even lower stratum of demoralization than before, she had an unexpected visitor.

'But...I thought visiting hours...' was all that Janet could say as with distinctly mixed feelings she saw Margaret Llewellyn bearing down upon her.

'Nonsense, my dear, I've just spoken to Sister and it's perfectly all right,' said Margaret with a dismissive gesture of a lordly hand. 'You'll find a word in the right ear is all that's necessary in these cases. Miss Gray, the principal nursing officer, is a personal friend of mine, of course...' She left the sentence hanging in mid-air, implying that such plebeian things as hospital rules and ward visiting hours were made only for the observance of complete fools or those of lowly station in life.

Her voice, a great hearty plum pudding of a voice that would not be out of place reading the riot act to an undisciplined pack of foxhounds, was not noticeably lowered for talking to Janet, who was uncomfortably aware that most of the other patients in the ward were looking up from their papers and knitting to stare open-mouthed at the invader.

'It's...er...very nice of you to come,' she managed lamely, wondering whether there was any chance of her transport to X-ray turning up in the immediate future, say the next two minutes. Whatever horrors the IVP might involve, they could hardly be much worse than the acute embarrassment of a loud-voiced conversation in the middle of a hospital ward with Margaret at her most grande dame-ish.

'How ever did you know I was here?'

'Quite simple, my dear. I rang back

yesterday evening to ask you whether you wanted to borrow some sherry glasses for the refreshments after the committee meeting—' (sherry? thought Janet. You'll be lucky! They'll get coffee and sandwiches and like it)— 'and of course you weren't there, and dear Angus told me all about it. I must say he seems to be bearing up very well under the strain. I always think it's *so* much worse for the ones who are coping at home, don't you? Anyway he said you had this perfectly *dreadful* pain most of yesterday, and I said, "But I spoke to her on the phone only this afternoon and she was all right then," but he would insist that you were really quite ill, so after that of course I held my tongue. Anyway, they—' (the lordly hand waved vaguely in the direction of the office)— 'obviously think you are ill or you wouldn't be here. They're terribly short of beds, you know.'

Janet grinned weakly, nurturing unkind thoughts about the ground opening up to swallow Margaret Llewellyn, or herself or both.

'Now then,' the voice turned businesslike, if no quieter. 'How are they treating you? I can't say this ward seems a particularly suitable place for you. I think at least a single room—unless you prefer to be transferred to the private wing. When one is ill one needs someone to get things moving for one, don't you think? And public wards are so... so...well—' (she looked round at the occupants of the other beds, who were all promptly occupied with their magazines or knitting patterns again)— 'so very *public*, aren't they? A word in the right place, you know, it's easily arranged.'

Janet tried to protest that she had no complaints about her treatment so far, and that even though she had hardly been in the ward long enough to judge she saw no reason for wanting to move.

'Anyway,' she added firmly, hoping the audience round her would hear, 'I like the company.'

Apart from anything else she was not

going to let on to Margaret that the cost of private treatment was quite out of the question: such things as poverty, even relative poverty, only entered Margaret's experience in the context of fecklessness, mismanagement, or other forms of more-or-less culpable misfortune viewed, and frowned on, from the well-heeled security of her various do-good committees. Anyway she could not be trusted not to have a word in somebody's ear to sort out the financial implications as well, quite unaware of causing any humiliation to the recipient.

'By the way, my dear,' the voice changed again, this time to its county hostess tone, and a be-ringed hand came down on Janet's arm, for all the world as if she was being arrested in the act of something and was about to be marched off, '*who* is that doctor I saw in the office as I came in? A young man, so neatly turned out, nice looking, really rather presentable?'

'I don't know anything about him. But he seems to be the doctor who looks after this ward. The houseman, they call it, don't they? I think I heard someone say his name was Doyle. Why?'

'Doyle,' Margaret repeated. 'Doyle...' She said the name over several times as if it tasted strange. 'I think I know his mother,' she announced at last.

'Oh,' said Janet. There didn't seem much else to say.

'That's right. Velma Doyle, charming woman. I've met her several times, and I remember when we were talking at the Three Charities cocktail party she mention- ed she had a son who was a doctor here. I can see the likeness now I think about it. Well, at least you're in good hands in that respect. But I really think somewhere with a little more...well, privacy, don't you know?'

'I'm quite happy here,' Janet maintained stoutly, and slightly louder than necessary, praying this was not going to turn into some sort of public slanging match.

At that moment, praise be, like some

blessed *deus ex machina*, a porter appeared with a wheelchair to take Janet to X-ray.

Margaret Llewellyn clucked something disapproving, she didn't catch what, and promised (or threatened) to come again soon. Janet cordially hoped not, but the visit somehow left her feeling vaguely guilty at having in some way let the side down by being ill. She felt that *noblesse oblige*, usually one of Margaret's favourite expressions, would sooner or later have reared its ugly head if the conversation had gone on much longer.

The rest of the day, like so much of life in hospital, seemed to be spent waiting around. The porter left her in X-ray, where she scanned indifferently through a selection of torn women's magazines for twenty minutes or so until a girl, not much older than one of her own sons, made her discard her nightie in a cubicle and put on one of these ridiculous backless tie-less gowns designed by some hospital humorist to ensure a minimum of decency combined with a maximum of draught. After another twenty minutes' wait she was given some white fluid to drink out of a beaker, not actually unpleasant stuff but it brought a nasty aftertaste up into her throat. More delay, more dog-eared magazines, then a series of X-rays taken by a young chirpy girl who seemed far too bored with the whole procedure to explain what was actually happening or why; and Janet was by this time too depressed, hungry and cold to care anyway.

'Right, that's the last one,' said the girl at last. It was by now the middle of the afternoon. 'Oh, no, don't get changed yet. We want to be sure they've come out all right.' Janet waited, clasping her skimpy gown and anonymous towelling dressing-gown more closely round her. It appeared the last shot of the series was not all right and had to be taken again. Back into the bleak den with the big whirring monster. Another shot, and another wait. By now the ancient magazines had lost any charm they might once have had. How could just waiting around be so tiring and demoralizing? Janet wondered.

At long last she was back in her bed, slumped against the cool bank of welcoming pillows.

'How do you feel, dear?' the varicose veins over on her left enquired kindly.

'Flaked out,' she said, adding apologetically, 'I can't understand why.'

'At least you look a bit better than you did when they brought you in,' joined in a plump, cheerful-looking woman who was sitting up in a quilted bedjacket doing a crossword. 'You looked really poorly then. We could see you were in a lot of pain.'

'Yes, at least that's gone at the moment,' said Janet. 'At least I think it has.' After the brusque girls of X-ray had finished with her she was not really any too sure.

But she had at least been given a cup of tea and some buttered toast and had regained some of her morale an hour or so later when Bill Doyle appeared with a brown envelope of X-rays and perched informally on the edge of the bed (strictly against the rules, Janet suspected). He was a pleasant, well-groomed and well-spoken young man—just the sort of young man whose mother Margaret Llewellyn would make it her business to know, she reflected.

'Well, Mrs Dunbar, you've still got us guessing,' he said. 'From your symptoms and the tests so far we are ninety per cent certain the trouble is in your kidney, probably a stone. We hoped the IVP would settle the details for us. You see, what happens is that you drink the white milky stuff, and that contains a special substance that shows up on X-rays. We give it long enough to work through to your kidneys, then we X-ray them at pre-determined intervals and assess the progress of the material through your kidney. Anything that causes a hold-up, such as a stone or something wrong with the kidney, should show up.'

'And didn't it?'

'No.'

She was not sure whether she should be apologizing for remaining a problem, or feeling glad at keeping her clean bill of health intact.

'So what...well, what happens next?'

'You must stay here, of course, until we really get to the root of the trouble. We are still pretty certain it must be a stone. Don't worry, it's not unusual for them to fail to show up on X-rays when you want them to. Drink as much as you can in the hope that we can dislodge it, and we'll do another IVP in a few days' time. OK?'

He treated her to one of the vaguely amiable smiles he kept for female patients of as-yet-unassessed intelligence and wandered back up the ward.

Sister Blandish came to tell her roughly the same thing a while later, except that where Dr Doyle had managed to make it all sound like a secure and even rather enjoyable parlour game, Sister's gambit of, 'Well, there's nothing on the X-ray to account for this...pain of yours,' immediately made her feel on the defensive. An impostor of some kind in a ward full of genuine sufferers.

'Will I be here long?' she asked hesitantly. 'I'm worried about things at home...my husband...the boys.'

'How should *I* know, dear? They can't make a positive diagnosis without X-ray proof, now can they?' And the lack thereof was quite clearly Janet's own fault.

'Have you any pain at the moment?'

'No.'

'Well, that's good, anyway.' Unexpectedly, Sister gave her hand a reassuring pat. 'Don't worry, Mrs Dunbar, I'm sure they'll cope all right for a few days at home. We'll soon get you sorted out, and a bit of rest'll do you a world of good, anyway. You see.'

The sudden kindness demoralized poor Janet almost more than the preceding brusqueness, and she felt near to tears as she watched Blandish pause to speak to a group of patients round the table and then go back to the office. A wave of sudden misery and homesickness overtook her. She tried to find comfort in the fact that it would be visiting time soon. With any luck

Angus would come (please not that awful Margaret again).

And perhaps her kind Nurse Miniver would be on duty again tonight. Just the thought made her feel better and she reached determinedly for the tissue box on her locker.

CHAPTER FIVE

It was a busy morning for Jamie McTweed. No leisurely coffee breaks today—what with the big white chief bringing a worship of students on his morning round to gawp and fumble and generally upset the routine.

'Now, *Doctor* McTweed,' he would say in that dry, itchy voice of his. 'Tell us all about this new patient, if you please.' He always pronounced it *Doc*-tor when he addressed Jamie—at best meant to be mock-Scottish pronunciation derogating his country of origin, at worst a sarcastic emphasis on the title of doctor which he quite evidently felt his victim was unfit to bear. The 'if you please' part was just the way the old codger spoke, no matter who he was addressing.

He was in one of his showing-off moods

today, perhaps because he had a couple of the research students from the Postgraduate Centre on the round as well as his registrar, Dr Magnus Whitehorn, the research maniac. To Dr Whitehorn the research students were a happy stimulus to argument, so that these rounds could entail hours of endless theoretical cut-and-thrust at the bedside of each bewildered and uncomprehending patient. Not only did Jamie have to do a special round after they had gone reassuring each of his worried charges that the wealth of long words and statistics did not necessarily spell out imminent doom; but each diagnostic sparring match, each matching of medical wits meant that more and remoter tests were needed for the proof of refutation of each increasingly exotic theory. And guess whose job it would be to organize (or look up in the textbooks and then organize) these tests, follow through the fate of the different specimens and have the results on hand for next time.

He somehow felt like an old-fashioned

yokel on Dr Brian Dickory's medical estate…Yessir, he should be saying respectfully, Thank ee sir, only too glad of a bit more work sir, oh no, four hours of sleep a night suits me well enough, thank ee sir, pulling his forelock and resenting in silence the while.

Somehow he had to stick this job out, however much he detested it, somehow keep his nose clean and his record unsullied for the remaining weeks in the post. How many weeks was it anyway? he started wondering. How many days, hours, minutes? It was like at school counting till the end of term. Perhaps he should have a chart on his wall, or notches on the bare little bedstead in his digs. Or would female visitors misconstrue this as a score of a different kind? That might be interesting. What would hard-to-get Staff Nurse Mackie with the comely ankles and the pert line in backchat make of an apparent score of fifteen or twenty carved out of the deal headboard? Decide she must be missing something after all, or run a mile (perhaps even displaying knees as comely as the ankles in her flight...)? How would Mousie Miniver react?

'Well, *Doctor* McTweed, what do you think?'

Oh hell, I hadn't been listening to a word. How long had the dogfight been going on happily without him?

'I'm sorry, sir? I was just checking this, er...' What was there in that bundle of notes in his hand that he might conceivably have been checking, he wondered.

Not for the first time one of the more self-righteous students came to his rescue, glad of every opportunity to chalk up a point in a competitive game.

'Seventy-eight, sir.'

Usually Jamie cursed their all-knowing smugness. They had nothing better to do than swot up in advance on the kind of questions the boss and the bickering researchers were likely to spring, and leap in smartly with quick answers, wrong-footing the poor houseman who had the clinical work for a wardful of patients to do and had quite often been up two or three times during the previous night doing it. This time, however, Jamie wafted a silent thankyou in the crawler's direction.

He was not, however, off the hook yet.

'And do you agree with the opinion of your rather precocious colleague, *Doctor* McTweed?'

Hell again, if he knew what the question was he might stand a better chance. This was one you could not win, like Have you stopped beating your wife.

He would have to take a gamble, and judging by the patness with which the answer came out and that particular student's track record for accuracy, he said: 'Yes, I do, sir,' with all the certainty he could muster, and a prayer to the patron saint of housemen that he might sound as if he had *some* idea of what he was supposed to be talking about. 'Seventy-eight.'

'That seems a very reasonable estimate,' agreed Hickory Dickory. 'Eighty to eighty-five in extreme cases. Over eight-five—' he shook his head. (Jamie never did find out seventy-eight what.)

His voice was dry as fallen leaves, his face unsmiling—or was there, as he looked at Jamie, the slightest suggestion of a twinkle in his eyes?

'You see, gentlemen,' he turned on the pack of white coats at his heels with a fierceness that made the keenest two or three in the front fall back a pace or so, 'how quickly a good doctor can collect his wits in an emergency. You thought perhaps that Dr McTweed here was daydreaming. Perhaps *I* even thought that Dr McTweed was daydreaming.' An ill-timed snigger from the back of the squad won a piercing glare. In the silence that followed Jamie wondered what on earth he could be leading up to. Never again, he vowed, would he let his mind wander during these wretched rounds.

'But perhaps,' H-D was going on, 'there are things we do not always remember to take into account. Dr McTweed, when were you last officially off duty?'

'The evening before last, sir, on call again as from midnight.'

'How many times were you called that night?'

'Only once, sir.'

'Only once. Thank you.' He paused, like Counsel allowing the jury a while to digest some particularly dramatic titbit of evidence. 'Comparatively quiet. And last night how many calls were there between, say, eleven o'clock and seven?' Jamie began to sense, with a pleasant glow, that the wind had somehow changed, and that for some reason far beyond his comprehension he had changed from being the dunce of the hour to being some sort of hero.

'Four, sir.' Then he added with what was meant to come across as a winning streak of modesty, 'But one was a false alarm, no, two of them were really.'

'Would you care to be more precise, Doctor?'

'At about midnight I was called to admit a coronary who went up to the ICU under Dr Garretty. At two-fifteen a lad was admitted in a coma. It turned out he was only twelve and paediatrics came out in force and took him off my hands. Then at about three o'clock the chap in the side ward had his CVA and I was called. Not that there was much I could do. You saw him just now, sir. Mr Joddrey.'

'Yes, yes.' Hickory Dickory was probably about to continue his homily, but Jamie pretended not to notice.

'And about half an hour after that I was called again—' he paused just long enough to emphasize but not unduly labour the point— 'because night sister was under the impression I had gone off to bed with the DDA book.'

'And had you?'

Triumphantly: 'No, sir.'

The case rests, my lord.

'You see, gentlemen,' under the boss's beady eyes the few remaining sniggers had turned into respectful coughs, 'while you were all safe and warm in your beds in the arms of Morpheus, or whoever else's arms it was—' nobody dared venture more than a respectful smile at this— 'this staunch young member of your noble profession was struggling on, making do on, what, nine hours' sleep out of the forty-eight. You have either forgotten what it was like, or you have it to come, gentlemen, you have it to come.'

The group continued in a chastened mood, except for Jamie who felt a bubble of self-righteous elation floating gaily inside him and buoying him up. One or two of the students even eyed him with something approaching respect, which was something he never thought to see, and Mackie treated him to a wink as she headed off about her business when at last, some centuries later, the round broke up.

Perhaps life was not so bad after all, he mused, and to prove it he would think up some pretext for visiting the outer of the principal nursing officer's sacred precincts and chat up Selina.

She was at her desk, looking, to the untrained eye, for all the world as if she was doing some work. The trained eye might have spotted the slightly open desk drawer with the open paperback lying ready just inside, or the eyebrow tweezers tucked hastily under the edge of the typewriter as footsteps approached. Jamie's eyes were far more interested in the sleek close-cropped cap of dark hair, the black long-lashed eyes and full scarlet mouth; the figure...now there was a figure that could have really done something for a nurse's uniform...or for a ward housekeeper's overall, come to that...or for almost anything. As it was, she was pushing out a tight sweater and skirt (mandatory office uniform) in a not uninteresting way...

' 'Ullo, Jamie.' The voice with its raw edge of accent came as a shock even to the devoted Jamie. ' 'Ow's tricks, then?'

'Not bad,' he said. 'Not bad at all. Remind me to tell you about this morning's round with Hickory Dickory.'

' 'Ere, look what I've got, Jamie.' Almost everything she had got was mouth-wateringly evident as she got up from her chair and wiggled her tightly clad form round to the filing cabinet. She held out two large printed cards.

Instinctly sensing disaster, Jamie's heart sank.

'What are they?'

'*What are they?* They're only what everyone in the hospital is after, tickets to Matron's Ball.'

'Oh.'

'Why, is that all you can say, Oh?'

'How did you get them?'

'Well, although the Friends of the Hospital do most of the organisation, we have to 'elp with the secretarial work and since it involves quite a lot of overtime, they give us tickets. Kind of perks, you might say. You'll take me, won't you. You'll 'ave to take me, Jamie, please.'

'And how do you think I can pay for those

tickets? I've hardly two—'

But a long scarlet talon was pointing out the overprinting that went diagonally across the card, COMPLIMENTARY.

'There,' she triumphed. 'And don't try on any of your nonsense about not having a dinner jacket like you did last year, and it turned out you had one at home in London all the time, because it's in fancy dress, so there.'

'Oh God,' said Jamie.

'It'll be great, I just know it will. Please, Jamikins,' she wheedled.

'Oh...I don't know...it depends on work. And you are *not* to call me that stupid childish name. I can't stand it.'

'All right, lover. You take me to Matron's Ball, and I'll never call you Jamikins again...Jamikins.'

'Oh...we'll see,' he said irritably. 'You know how difficult it is for me to plan things in advance.'

'Sure, I know. Eh, you're not going, are you? I've got my lunch break in five minutes.'

'Yes, I've got to dash,' he lied. 'We're pretty tied up this morning and I really just came in to borrow a few of those little green tags you always have such a supply of. The ward's right out and stationery don't seem to have any till tomorow. Thanks. See you.'

Irritating girl, sometimes. Physically a wow. No denying that. Mentally about as exciting as breeding cardboard boxes—well, you couldn't have everything. And conversationally, quite distinctly abrasive at times. Why, even little Mousie Miniver didn't have *that* much of a capacity for getting on his nerves.

Mousie Miniver. His mind pondered the problem as he strolled towards the canteen. The project really wasn't to his liking, cash or no cash. The Selinas of the world, well they might be maddening at times, but one knew the score with them. It was all a game, hunter and hunted, and both players knew the rules so nobody got hurt. Start involving a girl like Mousie and there might be all sorts of complications and repercussions. Innocent, green creature that she was. Why, it wouldn't surprise him if she had never even...

Perhaps he could go back to Bob and the boys.

'I say, lads, I've been thinking about this. I don't think I'll go through with it after all. You know what they say about discretion being the better part of valour and all that sort of thing.'

He could hear Bob Scriven's reply, too. 'Of course. We understand, don't we, boys? He's just chickening out. All this fine talk of his is nothing but hot air,' and their mocking laughter echoed in his ears.

In this moment of indecision, the very last person he wanted to meet was Nurse Miniver herself. But there she was coming towards him down the corridor. Caught off balance, his first reaction was to try and pretend he had not seen her. But as they drew nearly level she gave him a shy smile, and some sort of reaction was necessary.

'Hallo, Mous—I mean Shirley.'

'Hallo.'

'Talk of the devil...'

'Oh?'

'Well, not talk exactly. What I mean is, what a coincidence bumping into you because I was just thinking about you.'

'Something nice, I hope.'

'Wondering if the coffee came out.'

'Oh, that. I put it to soak in one of those biological powders as soon as I took it off.'

'The ones that eat the material as well as the stain?'

'That's right. It's gone to the laundry now. I'm sure it'll be OK. Plenty worse things than coffee get spilt down a nurse's apron, after all.'

He wondered if she would be quite so much all-sweetness-and-light if she knew he had done it on purpose, and why.

She smiled again and started to walk on.

Quick, you fool, make some use of the situation. You won't get a chance like this again for days, perhaps never.

'I say—'

She paused and looked back, surprised.
For a second his mind went blank. What
were you supposed to say when you dated
nice girls, rather than picking up casual dates
at local hops or selecting a morsel of local
talent from among the casual drinkers at the
White Rabbit? For a moment his mind
zoomed back to shy sweaty-palmed and
acne-d days in the sixth form, but that would
never do either.

'What about you and me taking in a film?'

She looked surprised but quite pleased.

'I...I don't know. When?'

He thought quickly. 'Tomorrow evening?'

'Well, I have got tomorow evening off...'

Some male decisiveness was required.

'Good. I'll meet you in Leicester Square
at seven o'clock.'

Still she hesitated.

'Of course, if you've got a date already,
don't let me...'

That did the trick.

'No,' she said. 'And of course, I'd like

to come.'

'Good. I look forward to it,' he lied.

He found he was thinking ahead, planning. What part of the cinema was best? The front gave you eye-strain but was cheap. The back of the stalls had obvious advantages but might arouse her suspicions and put her on her guard. Should he take her some chocolates? A corny gesture, but the sort of thing that might impress her, which was the object, after all.

And since he had decided to go ahead with the project it obviously had to be taken seriously.

But just to prove to himself that everything was still normal underneath the trite boy-meets-girl facade, he pinched Staff Nurse Mackie's pert little bottom in the ward corridor when he got back to Men's Medical. She slapped his face, predictably, and he felt better.

He was not due for a free evening the next day, so he had a word with Dinah Went. She was Dr Garretty's houseman and they quite often stood in for one another. She, being married, found the hours particularly trying.

'What are you up to this time, another evening of unmitigated vice in the notorious hell-holes of Titchford, or are you planning to make your fortune and buy your freedom from slavery at Larry's by beating the system at Babington Dog Track?' She had no illusions about him, friend Dinah. It didn't matter though. Even his list of possibilities did not include married women. Didn't need to.

'Ah,' he said mysteriously, 'would you believe me if I said I was taking a nice girl to the cinema?'

'Frankly, no. But I didn't expect the truth anyway. I lead a sheltered and respectable life and I might be shocked. I'll do you a deal. I'll take tomorrow evening for you if you'll take the third of next month for me. It's a Tuesday and our anniversary. We usually try to have some sort of a knees-up if I can get off.'

'It's a deal,' said Jamie.

'What are you going to see?'

'Haven't the foggiest.'

'Do you know something—that's the worst cover story I've heard for ages! Never mind, whatever, you're up to, don't do anything I wouldn't do—but if you do, mind you enjoy it.'

'OK, Dinah. Thanks.'

For better or worse. Operation Mousie Miniver was beginning to gather momentum.

Janet Dunbar was having a rotten day. The pain was back, perhaps not quite as bad as that first day at home before coming into hospital: or perhaps it seemed more bearable because she was in a warm bed in a ward being looked after, and the pain was in some remote and bleakly comforting way somebody else's responsibility, not hers. But it was bad enough. And the fact that the injections they gave her from time to time made her feel dizzy, sick and thoroughly miserable did not help. She was not even sure sometimes how long she had been in hospital—two days, three, four? Through the haze she could not remember for certain.

'Drink, dear, you must drink as much as you can,' was all they seemed to be able to say to her, refilling the plastic glass on her locker with unappetizing squash. A huge pot of tea, now, or an endless supply of coffee, that might have been a bit more encouraging. But she never fancied cold lemonade much even at home when the boys drank it.

She mentioned her nausea to Sister, who was not particularly sympathetic.

'Of course, if you'd rather have the pain...' she said.

'No, of course I wouldn't, it's a dreadful pain, and anything's better. But aren't there any other sorts of injection that work just as well?'

Sister considered her coldly for a moment.

'I'll speak to Dr Doyle,' she said.

Janet, too miserable even to resent the tone of voice, said nothing. Everyone she had mentioned her nausea to had said, 'I'm sure you shouldn't be feeling like that, have you told the nurses?' if they themselves were not nurses, or 'Have you told Sister?' if they were. A sister in a hospital ward was quite a little autocrat when you thought about it. It was easy to mock (when one was well and firmly on two feet, outside the hospital) at the extent to which patients and nurses alike always seemed to kow-tow to them, but once you were horizontal in here, more-or-less helpless and dependent on them, you realized just how much power they wielded in their little kingdoms and how easily they could make life difficult for those who did not get on with them.

Did anyone, Janet wondered, get on with Sister Blandish?

At that moment, had she but known it, Marion Blandish was less concerned with getting *on* with her patients or anyone else, than with trying to get *off* with Dr Bill Doyle in the relative seclusion of the ward office. He, poor fellow, had started off by making the tactical error of being discovered alone, seated and writing up patients' notes, and was now paying for his rashness by seeing la Blandish, eyes gleaming like some female Dracula scenting blood, advancing upon him.

'Ah, Dr Doyle. Bill.' The voice had a steely seductiveness to it. 'There you are. I wonder if you would mind signing these forms.'

'Of course. What are they?' He remained casually cheerful, hoping he was mistaken about the slightly lowered eyelids, the slightly pouting lips.

'The test for occult blood in Mrs Bickley's stools. 'Not a good line to try and say sexily, but to give her her due, she made the best she could of it.

She walked across to him slowly with a sway which in a short-skirted sixteen-year-old might have been ingenuously attractive, leant across to put the form down in front of him and stayed bent over him to watch him write. Her thigh was pressed unambiguously against his shoulder.

He signed quickly.

'There you are,' he said brightly, hoping she would go away.

She did not go away, but stayed there, quite deliberately pressing against him. She was wearing perfume, not too much of it, but uncomfortably, muskily, overwhelming at such close quarters. He tried to shift across in the chair but was too close to the wall.

He was trapped. Stay cool at all costs.

'I was, er, just looking through these X-rays of Mrs Dunbar's again,' he said. 'We'll do another IVP tomorrow.'

'She needs a different painkiller; the pethidine makes her sick.'

Her hand rested lightly on his shoulder. He tried to ignore it.

'Right-ho, I'll, er, just make a note of that, Sister. D-u-n-b-a-r different analgesic. There.'

'Don't call me Sister. Not when we're alone like this. Call me Marion.'

'All right, Marion. You see, there's something here, that tiny shadow, that could have been overlooked and just might turn out to be what we're looking for.'

He made as if to hold the plate up against the light, but her hand held his arm gently but insistently down.

'I know what *I'm* looking for, Bill, and it's flesh and blood, not X-ray plates.'

'It's the smallest of shadows,' he struggled on, 'but—'

'Why must we always talk shop, you and me?' the thigh moved, provocatively against his shoulder.

'Well, being a doctor and a nurse...I mean a sister...'

'But we're human beings too, Bill. With bodies, and feelings. And here we are alone together...surely you must realize how I feel about you?'

'Well, I...'

He racked his brains for the best way out of this, quite literal, corner.

'You mustn't be shy, you know. Not with me. I know I'm professionally your senior, and perhaps I'm even a year or two older than you. But I'm a woman first, with a woman's needs, can't you see that?'

It was not just the pressure of her body against him. Her hand had travelled round and was easing its way in through the undone button below his tie.

Spurred by desperation, Bill Doyle adopted the only escape tactic he could think of. He pushed the little wooden chair smartly backwards and stood up, nipped nimbly round the blue-clad figure and made for the door. Marion Blandish grabbed at the edge of the desk to keep her balance, and it was not love but fury that blazed from her eyes when she turned. But Bill was not waiting for any more. Muttering something ridiculous about an appointment he had forgotten he bolted with undignified haste for the ward, people and safety.

He wished when he thought back on the episode, that he could forget the undertones in her voice suggesting solitary walks through Titchford to while away drab off-duty hours, too spotless a room in the sister's corridor of the nurses' home, too regular an attendance in the hospital canteen. But dammit, the woman's loneliness was no concern of his! And if he could not laugh the episode off quite as easily as he would have liked, neither was there going to be *any risk* whatever of it happening again.

So it was that he began to consort somewhat more closely than was usual with another member of the more senior nursing staff on the ward. As it worked out, as well as being the next in command, she was also amenable, generally friendly and totally unlikely to misconstrue his attentions. It was that funny little non-person of a staff nurse who had just come off nights, the one they all nicknamed Mousie Miniver. And while a houseman cannot actually *ignore* the sister on a ward where he works, with a knowledgeable, obliging, and uncritical staff nurse to relay requests, instructions and queries, he can (and did) come pretty close to it.

And so it was that when Margaret Llewellyn next came to visit her dear friend Janet Dunbar, the first thing she noticed on entering the ward was Dr Doyle (Velma Doyle's boy, don't you know, and *such* a nice young man) deep in conversation with that sweet little staff nurse Janet was always praising to the skies. They looked so right as a pair, my dear.

'I know I'm an incurable romantic,' the tweedy Llewellyn confessed to her rather surprised friend, 'but I always think doctors and nurses should marry each other, don't you? There is something so fitting about it, somehow.'

'Well, those two certainly seem as thick as thieves,' said Janet. The two had by now finished consulting over the results of Mrs Bickley's latest tests and were on opposite sides of the ward, about their separate business. It may be that Bill Doyle kept an eye on where his new ally had got to in case he should need rescuing in an emergency, his nerves being somewhat shattered after his recent experience; but in any case Janet's casual remark had been enough to stir the doughty imagination that lurked, along with the romantic heart, under Margaret Llewellyn's leathery exterior.

'You can see how he looks at her across the ward,' she pronounced. 'Of course *I* could tell the moment I walked into the ward. People in love generate a sort of electricity, don't they? I wonder if Velma knows. I can't wait to tell her.' A new thought struck her. 'You're sure this girl is quite...suitable, aren't you?'

'I hadn't really thought about it. I know she's the best nurse I've ever come across, sympathetic and —'

'Yes, dear, I'm sure she is. That wasn't *quite* what I meant. *I* mean can she speak the Queen's English and use the right knife and fork at dinner? Frankly, dear, is she one of *us*?'

Oh, do go away, you silly snobbish old windbag, thought Janet. You try feeling as ill as this and see how much the social accomplishments of the nurses matter to you then. What matters is whether they give you a friendly smile when they come on duty and whether they can give you an injection without making you leap out of the bed.

'Yes, I'm sure she is,' she answered in a tired voice.

'You're not at all well, are you, dear? Here, I've brought you some grapes. Oh, these dreadful plastic bowls! Still, I suppose it's the best they've got. That's the trouble with the Welfare State, everything's so shoddy. You'd be much better off as a private patient, you know. I do wish you'd let me have a word with my friend, Miss Gray. Anyway—' she consulted a large man's wrist watch on her large wrist— 'I must go now. Love you and leave you, as they say. Oh, and by the way, don't worry about the committee meeting, I've got it *all* organized. Dear Margo Melbourne is going to have it at her house.'

At last she was gone, sensible crepe-soled shoes squeaking the lino all the way to the ward door.

Janet lay back in bed exhausted, wishing the world would go away, with Dr Doyle, Staff Nurse Miniver and Margaret Llewellyn.

CHAPTER SIX

Shirley Miniver had always been the odd one out. She was resigned to it continuing to be the pattern of her life. She had an elder brother and a younger sister. The younger sister, Julie, had always been a pretty little thing (that was people's description of her, ever since Shirley could remember, A Pretty Little Thing) with fair curls and blue eyes just like a little girl ought to look. She had a wilful temper and took shameless advantage of the spoiling the baby of the family inevitably receives.

John, the eldest of the three, was quiet and studious, but with good looks of the slightly fragile sort that girls found irresistible and he always seemed to be bringing home pretty girls.

Shirley was the plain one. All her life she had known it, though nobody had ever once told her she was plain, or ever needed to. Other girls were told how pretty they looked tonight. *She* was complimented on the colour of her dress, on how neatly she had plaited her hair or on how well-manicured her hands were, never on the overall effect which she knew was drab. Nobody suggested how she could do anything about it and presumably there was nothing to be done. And while she had all sorts of compensating virtues like being patient and kind and generous-hearted almost to a fault, they were no compensation to her. All she could do was shelter behind her glasses as best she could and put a brave face on it.

When John had his twenty-first birthday, their parents gave him a dance, quite a sumptuous affair with friends of his from University coming and being parked out with obliging friends in the village for the night. One or two of them danced with her out of courtesy, another was obviously detailed to do so. In each case, aware of her lack of attraction, she was tongue-tied and clumsy and they quickly abandoned her for brighter company. Many teenagers have been through such miseries, spending whole evenings haunting the powder rooms and foyers to avoid being the consistent wallflower, and been consoled by fond mums and told that it would not last for ever.

Shirley had no such consolation and knew better than to seek it. Like every other girl she knew the story of the Ugly Duckling. But she in her gentle resigned way had no illusions. She knew that the ugly duckling grew up to be an ugly duck and all she could do was to make the best of it.

The pattern of social life at St Lawrence's proved much as she had always known it. Other girls had their dates, their flirtations, even their scandals, and she, who was popular among her colleagues as that rarest of birds, the good listener, enjoyed it all vicariously. But she got no joy at first hand. The other girls got engaged, married and left nursing, or broke off their liaison with tantrums and dramas. Shirley was happy for them, wished them well, or listened and resisted offering advice. She herself had two, perhaps three, casual dates in the time she was training. Certainly no more.

It would be a grievous exaggeration to say that she had ever wept into her pillow over Jamie McTweed. She had wept into her pillow a few times, but over the general cruelty of life, not over anybody specific. She knew Jamie McTweed well enough; at a distance, like she knew a dozen other young housemen. He was good-looking in the extrovert assured sort of way that Shirley had always most admired and envied. Her brother's handsomeness was something fortuitous, a pleasant trick of fate that always puzzled him slightly. Jamie, on the other hand, seemed to flaunt his good looks, enjoy them and use them to full advantage, like a young heir who had always known that wealth was to be his and was enjoying his inheritance to the utmost. It must be wonderful to be so sure of yourself; to be able to take your pick of all the pretty girls around and approach them without fear of a rebuttal.

When he bought her a coffee after that accident in the canteen, it was all so sudden she had not time to be awkward, and shy as she usually was. And, rather to her surprise, he had not been difficult to talk to either. He had seemed rather friendly, and had said one or two kind things that she had cherished since then. And his voice, with its slight Scots purr, had quite set her heart pounding.

She had been glad when his bleep called him away. She needed to savour that precious quarter-hour, remember and chew it over, mentally fix it before the colours ran and blurred. This was her ideal sort of man—not someone as plain as herself who danced one dance and wandered away, bored; and not a doctor who just talked to her on a professional level without so much as noticing her as a person—and he had for those few fine minutes been sitting there opposite her drinking a cup of coffee and chatting to her for all the world as if she was worth sitting down with and chatting to. Her poor atrophied morale had bloomed.

But now this. This was something different altogether.

At first it seemed too good to be true. He had actually invited her, *her,* to go out with him, for an evening, to the cinema. It was not just any old date, that was event enough in her life. It was this marvellous good-looking dashing dreamboat of a man. Just wait till she told the other girls...let them do some listening for a change...!

But then she started thinking. It would take all her courage to meet this man at a predetermined time, in cold blood. And in her heart she knew only too well what would happen. The old familiar story. Aware of her own lack of attractiveness, she would be self-conscious, gauche and boring. She was intelligent enough to know this, and sensitive enough to suffer desperately accordingly.

135

This made her more tense and self-conscious and the vicious circle grew tighter. If she was lucky he, because he was kind, would carry the evening. But behind that melting, easy-going smile, and that lighthearted chat he was so good at, he would be thinking of all the pretty, sexy and amusing girls he could have been out with instead.

Why wasn't he? Why should he have chosen to invite her? With all the good-timers to choose from, the gay, pretty ones, the sexpots, why her? Some odd form of slumming, perhaps—seeing how the ugly half lived? A joke, perhaps, and she herself presumably the butt of it? He didn't seem the spiteful type, but who could tell? She could not make it out. Puzzle as she might, it simply did not add up.

But she came to one conclusion. The idea of the evening scared her half to death. She did not want to make a fool of herself with him. She did not want that precious quarter of an hour in the canteen, ruined in retrospect. Fine unattainable star that he was, it was far better that he should stay un-attainable, twinkling safely up there in her sky. At a distance.

She stood him up. She actually stood him up! Little Mousie Miniver—how dare she! Half the girls in that hospital would have given their eye teeth for a date with him, good-looking debonair Jamie McTweed. He could usually take his choice. And she—a daft, plain little creature who ought to be grateful for anyone looking twice in her direction—actually threw away the chance and didn't deign to show up.

He had never felt so foolish as he did that evening, sitting on the bench in Leicester Square watching the world go by and waiting for her. Worse, being seen waiting for her. He did not wait around for girls: they waited for him. But he actually waited for her, for a while anyway. He felt a double idiot because after a lot of debating with himself he had reluctantly decided that the silly creature would probably be pleased if he acted up to the occasion a bit, and he had dragged himself into a shirt instead of the overworked sweater he usually wore off duty. A shirt and a tie under a reasonably respectable jacket. And he sat there praying Bob and the others would not see him. He would have been the laughing stock of the hospital and he knew it. As if they were not getting enough free mirth from his predicament without making things worse.

So there he sat like something stuffed waiting for this girl who never appeared. At first he felt angry at the personal affront, then upset at the waste of a rare carefully-manoeuvred free evening. Then puzzled. Had he played his cards wrong? Was it something he had said? Was the old charm slipping?

In the end he gave up. It was too late now for their visit to the cinema (no random suggestion, this. Everyone knew it was the best way of taking a girl out without having to talk to her all evening) and anyway he was not going looking for the wretched creature.

There were limits, quite apart from the fact that it would have needed at least a battalion of the Seventh Cavalry with bugles blowing and colours flying to force their way past Home Sister's office and into the nurses' quarters, and even then he did not know her room number.

Perhaps after all he could salvage the evening by a trip out to the Babington Dog Track. That should please Dinah Went. What was the time? Blast, it was too late. By the time he got there he would have missed all but the last couple of races. And anyway, what was the point if he had no spare cash to bet with?

Perhaps he would resort to the little red diary and chase up a few neglected favourites among the phone numbers. Two snags here: first, he was not going to change out of his best bib and tucker now, and none of the girls who got star billing in the little red diary were used to him in anything other than sweater and jeans, and he was not in the mood for their mirth; second, they might not be free, even to him, at such short notice and he didn't fancy any more rejections, however un-personal, in one evening.

He was, in fact, though he wouldn't admit it, feeling a bit sensitive altogether.

Blast her eyes! How dare she treat him like that!

He settled for a thoroughly disgruntled evening in his room, playing jazz too loud on the record player, dawdling through an old copy of *Sporting Life* he had had some fish and chips in, opening and eating cold a large tin of baked beans: and throwing darts at some salacious magazine's idea of a love goddess (probably stuffed as full of silicone implants as a teddy bear with flock) pinned up on the wall over the drab deal dressing-table. 'What about the wallpaper, Dr McTweed?' the landlady would say in her fussy-cum-motherly way when she saw the damage next time she cleaned the room. Well, what *about* the wallpaper? Call it fair wear and tear and send the bill in to the hospital. After all it was one of their miserable nurses he was really throwing darts at, not old Bulgy Boobs there. And some of the darts were landing with stunning accuracy in areas where prissy young staff nurses would much prefer they didn't.

He'd have a few smart words to say to Miss Mousie Miniver the next time he saw her. So help him, he would.

Or would have done if she hadn't still been his ticket to a precious thirty quid.

One thing was for sure. After the way she had treated him this evening there was going to be no more nonsense about her being A Nice Girl, no more qualms about Treating Her This Way. She was obviously as devious and wilful, self-centred and illogical as the rest of her sex. They were all the same, not above fighting foul when it suited them, and fair game for Jamie or any other man. It was full-scale war now.

He wanted that thirty pounds and he wanted it quickly. As far as he was concerned it was gloves off now, and the devil take the hindmost.

Janet Dunbar had been a patient for eight days now and was cordially sick of hospital and everything to do with it. Occasional episodes of severe pain were interspersed with hours of boredom and frustration and the feeling, familiar to anyone with hospital existence, that the time scale there was somehow quite different from those in the normal world. The whole perspective of existence was different. The newspaper told of wars and rumours of wars, floods, famines and football sensations; wife-swapping continued unabated in the wilds of Penge and beauty queens vamped bald-headed vicars. Angus and the boys somehow jolted along from one domestic crisis to the next, seeking only occasional advice on things that only a mother could know (like where is the twine to go with the stunter kite, last used two years ago, or what do you use to get chewing-gum off football socks?). But for Janet the scale of life was different. Mealtimes were the pinnacles of existence, the visit of the paperman or the Friends' trolley or the library were major events in the day.

That morning, the woman with the varicose veins, supplied with spare bandages and elastic support stockings, had been sent home after a round of such copious and heartfelt farewells you would think they had all spent a fortnight in the same holiday camp. Mrs Mace, with all the drainage pipes, actually managed her first short walk along the ward, shuffling palely between two nurses, her drainage bag pinned firmly to her dressing-gown, and these two events assumed such importance in the overwhelmingly boring pattern of the ward's existence that Janet actually found herself describing them in some detail to her family, as if they were major happenings and close friends.

As far as Janet was concerned, sweet nothing ever seemed to happen. She was taking some sort of tablet which Dr Doyle had told her was meant to dissolve the stone they all seemed so sure was there. And if anyone came and told her to drink as much as she could just once more, she was resolved to pour the contents of the water jug over them.

This morning, as it turned out, she was not feeling too bad. Not much pain, even the distinct stirrings of an appetite. She toyed with the possibilities of what might be for lunch. Meat? Shepherds pie? Her mouth was definitely watering, and Flo in the green overall had not even come round yet with her clattering trolley of cutlery and cruets. They had all written out their menu cards the day before, but the dishes promised seemed to bear singularly little resemblance to anything that actually turned up on the trays. One day, feeling brave, Janet had put a tick, more out of curiosity than appetite, against Beef Olives on the menu. What appeared had in fact borne more resemblance to shop-bought sausage rolls than any beef olive she, or anyone else in the ward, had ever come across. At the moment, she reflected, she felt hungry enough even to fancy *that*.

But it was not to be. A few minutes later, almost simultaneously with Flo laying the centre table and putting out the trays for the bed patients, along came one of the nurses with the dreaded NIL BY MOUTH card which she propped prominently on Janet's bedtable.

'Sorry, love, no dinner today.' She grinned unapologetically. 'And nothing more to drink for the time being.'

'But you nurses seem to spend most of your waking hours bullying me to drink more,' objected Janet irritably. 'Now you come and take my jug away.'

'I'm sorry, it's what Sister said. Another IVP.'

'That's hospital logic for you, dearie,' grinned Mrs Mace, who with the return of the use of her legs seemed to have rediscovered a sense of humour and a rather loud voice to give it vent. 'They tell you to drink but don't let you have any water. Sister giveth and Sister taketh away.'

'Blessed be the name of Sister—I don't

think,' added the teenager with wisdom-tooth problems, who after various complications was now fit and due to go home.

'Ssshhh,' said the nurse.

'No, love, it's not at all like that,' volunteered a green-robed theatre porter who had come to collect an operation patient and was idling by his trolley outside the drawn curtains of his intended passenger while a nurse vanished to check some detail or other. 'You know and I know that the Health Service has got to economize. Starving the patients is just the latest way of doing it. Stands to reason,' he added optimistically.

'Oh, I don't think that can be right,' joined in a girl with a carbuncle on her neck, who had been admitted into the varicose veins lady's bed. She seemed to be a student of some kind. 'You see, all these tests and things they do to people in hospital are terribly expensive; I've read about it in the papers. It would probably work out cheaper to feed you.'

That killed the conversation dead. The nurse whipped back the curtains drawn round the theatre patient as if she was about to produce a magic show, and the porter duly wheeled the gowned figure off; the student went back to drawing complicated diagrams in her notebook; and Janet was left contemplating the depressing prospect of no lunch and another grim spell in X-ray in the afternoon.

At least Sister was off duty from lunchtime, though she always seemed strangely reluctant actually to *go*, unlike most of the nurses who could not wait. Her (eventual) absence always signalled a certain relaxation among everyone on the ward. Nurses were more cheerful, less desperate to appear to be working every minute of the day, more at liberty to pause for a friendly word and a joke with the patients, even a proper heart-to-heart sometimes. And the patients themselves felt somehow more optimistic about their problems and less likely to grumble among themselves or try to escape in books or magazines. The television in the day room was turned a fraction louder without anyone complaining, there was more laughter at the meal table in the middle of the ward, and there was a noticeable, welcome, slackness about the rules concerning times and numbers of visitors.

Staff Nurse Miniver was on duty today, and *she* had even been known to offer visitors a cup of tea and to allow young children in to visit, bringing unexpected happiness into some mother's drab day.

She was on her way back up the ward after talking to the toothy teenager about her transport home the next day when she paused for a few minutes to chat with Janet.

'Sister was saying something about you wanting to be moved,' she said. 'Is there anything wrong? Because if it's anything we can put right—'

She perched in a friendly fashion near the foot of the bed, half sitting on the coloured counterpane, strictly against the rules, as Janet knew.

'I gather there was a phone call from Miss Gray's office, but I didn't quite understand *why* you wanted to be transferred.

'I don't. You're all marvellous. I've no complaints. Well, I mean to say...'

'It's all right. I quite understand.'

'It was all some sort of misunderstanding anyway. *I* certainly never asked for anything of the sort. I'm very grateful for what you're all doing.'

'Which at the moment is precious little, I'm afraid. By the way, the idea with these IVPs is to do one every few days and then compare them to try and get a clue where the stone is and whether it's actually moving. The spells of pain you get are probably caused by contractions of the muscle trying to squeeze it out, you see.'

'To be honest, I'm glad you believe I do get the pain. Lying here, like now, when there isn't any real pain, I feel such a fraud.'

'Don't you worry, Mrs Dunbar. Nobody who has suffered this particular pain, and it's not uncommon, would ever accuse you of being a fraud. It's said to be one of the worst pains around, renal colic. And you know—'

She was looking up the ward. Janet followed her eyes, hoping it was the porter to take her to X-ray. Beaten again. It was Margaret. Was there time, she wondered, to get Nurse Miniver to send her away, on the pretext that she was not up to seeing visitors? But it was too late. The tweedy apparition was almost upon them, waving cheerily and obviously quite unaware of being less-than-one-hundred-per-cent welcome.

'Hallo again,' she boomed. 'Still here, eh? So this is your charming young friend, is it?' She considered Shirley for a few seconds. 'Mmmm,' she pronounced, doctor-like, as if she had picked up medical mannerisms from her surroundings. 'No, don't go, Staff Nurse,' she ordered, and Shirley paused. 'Now tell me, my dear,' a well-meaning but somewhat crushing arm landed round the slim shoulder preventing escape. 'How much are you seeing of a certain young houseman at this hospital?'

'Margaret, you can't ask her *that!* What business is it of yours? You *can't* just go round quizzing people about their private lives!'

'*I* can.'

Shirley, open-mouthed with astonishment, stood looking from one to the other, silent.

'Everything is my busines that I choose to make my business, Janet, dear. Now, you've got more good sense than to be offended when I want to talk to you for your own good, haven't you, girl?'

'Well, I—'

'That's right. Let me put my question a bit differently. When was your off duty, yesterday?'

'In the evening.' There was no harm in humouring the woman; however objectionable she seemed, she was presumably one of Mrs Dunbar's friends, and *she* was pleasant enough.

'And did a certain young houseman, a rather good-looking pleasant lad altogether, ask you out? Don't be surprised, my dear. I can add two and two together.'

'And make five, apparently,' commented Janet angrily from the bed.

'He asked me, but if you really want to know, I didn't go. Now if you'll please excuse me.'

'You didn't go! But that's terrible.'

'Margaret, please!'

'Now you see here, young lady. I may be an old warhorse, but I know what I'm talking about. You have all the fun you can while you're young, all work and no play, you know how the saying goes. And I have good reason to think,' she tapped her nose knowingly, 'that that young man is very fond of you, perhaps more than you realize.'

Flustered and thoroughly put out, Shirley was only too glad to be rescued at that moment by a junior nurse requiring the medicine-cupboard keys. She escaped with relief.

Half an hour later the porter who came to take Janet in her wheelchair to X-ray found

her distressed and angry and looking dag
gers down the ward at the broad, totally
imperturbable, departing back of Margaret
Carruthers Llewellyn. They had just come
the closest they had ever come to a down-
right open row.

'If she's gone and upset that sweet little
Nurse Miniver, I'm going to kill her next
time I see her,' muttered Janet furiously to
nobody in particular.

If Nurse Miniver was upset she was good
at not showing it. But she was perhaps a little
quieter than usual for the rest of the afternoon.

CHAPTER SEVEN

Accustomed as he was to fielding the coronaries rushed to Casualty, Jamie had no reason to be suspicious of this one. Until he saw the patient, that was. He was called to Casualty to admit a medical case, an elderly man who collapsed in the street, with, apparently, all the right pains in all the right places, and been dashed in by ambulance. No letter, no history to go on, nothing. Except that he was in severe pain, and pale, as white as the pillow he was propped against on the trolley.

'I've had pain around that area before,' he told Jamie. 'Just suspected the old ticker wasn't all it might be...didn't want to ask for trouble by going to the quack...just be told to take it easy and all that nonsense anyway…but it's never been quite like this before…or this bad…'

He was wrapped in a scarlet ambulance blanket. Somewhere at about waist-level the whole blanket appeared to be throbbing, fast and regularly, as if there was a huge pulse directly underneath it. Jamie's heart sank.

'I'm just going to have a look at you,' he said, turning back the blanket gingerly, only too well aware what would be underneath.

The whole area just below the ribs was swollen, firm and throbbing in pulse time. If possible the man was even paler than a few minutes earlier. Jamie had only once before seen a case this bad, but it was one diagnosis that unfortunately even he could have no doubt about.

He carefully replaced the blanket and reached out for the drug chart, wrote up a generous *stat* dose of morphine and grabbed a nurse to get it organized as soon as possible. He added further morphine p.r.n. to the chart, but knew it was unlikely to be needed.

'Does your wife know you're here?'

'She's...on her way. Nurse...phoned... Doc, this is bad, isn't it? Am I...Am I going to...?'

'I don't know,' Jamie lied manfully. In his student days he had been so sure that a straight answer to a straight question was the kindest way. Nowadays he was not always so certain. What was so humane about depriving a man of hope?

On his way to the telehone a belligerent-looking Casualty sister blocked his way.

'You are, of course, putting that patient under intensive care,' she said. Jamie had not crossed swords with her so far in her short reign on Casualty, but her reputation for knowing better than SHOs, let alone common-or-garden housemen, was well established and he had a feeling he was about to now.

'I am of course doing no such thing, Sister,' he said firmly but politely, walking her out of earshot of the cubicle.

'That patient should be referred to the surgial firm on take and admitted as a matter of urgency to Intensive Care in preparation for emergency surgery.'

'That patient is dying and should be allowed to do so with as much dignity and as little fuss as possible.'

They stood in the middle of Casualty glaring at each other. Nurses turned to gape. Patients waiting on the end benches pricked up their ears at the raised voices.

By common consent they went into the office.

'I'm ringing Dr Whitehorn about this,' said Sister, picking up the phone.

'Be my guest,' said Jamie, cold with anger. Interfering old busybody. At least he knew Whitehorn would back his decision every inch of the way—they had discussed just this sort of case often enough to be sure of that.

Before she got through a short white-coated figure came into the office. It was the registrar of the surgical firm on take.

'Ah, Mr Trueman.' Sister stressed the 'Mr' in a slightly obsequious voice that made Jamie wince. 'Dr McTweed would like your advice on a case which has just come in. Needing emergency surgery, *I* would say,' she prompted.

Jamie said the least he civilly could until Mr Trueman had seen the patient and the three of them stood once more out of ear-shot of the cubicle.

'Mm, he could have had that for years,' mused Mr Trueman. 'Now it's leaking and probably due to rupture at any moment. Pity. No Sister, I'm sorry. No surgeon in his right mind would take on odds like that. A quiet medical bed somewhere, plenty of tender loving care...' he shrugged his shoulders wearily and turned away.

'But shouldn't we call Mr Blackwell...or at least Dr Dickory...?'

'Sister, you just call whoever you like, from Mr Blackwell to the Archangel Gabriel. But meanwhile I suggest you let Dr McTweed get on with admitting his patient to wherever he sees fit.' He strode off.

Jamie was about to go back into the cubicle when the nurse who had been in there came out.

'Doctor, I think...he's...'

Relief was Jamie's first reaction. Then he sighed. Now the paperwork would include a death certificate; and the already difficult-enough interview with the wife would now involve obtaining permission for a post-mortem as well as tactful news-breaking and attempts at consolation.

The interview proved as difficult as he had feared.

'He could have had this trouble for years,' he said, knowing it was not any help, but feeling he had to say something in the silence.

'Well, he never *said* anything, at least not to me,' she told her cup of tea, the hospital's standard attempt at solace at times like these. 'Honest, he never said a word about it.' A pale weeping figure in an anaemic-looking blue headscarf, she somehow seemed to be on the defensive.

'Well, at least he didn't suffer for very long,' seemed to be the formula under the circumstances. 'He had an injection for the pain, of course, and we did everything we could, but—'

'I'm sure you did, and I'm ever so grateful. It's just...' She blubbered unrestrainedly, spilling her tea. Jamie carefully took the cup from her and put it back in its saucer, then looked round helplessly for a box of tissues. They should be standard issue in interview rooms, or laid on routinely for difficult interviews, along with the tea tray.

'...It's just that...we had a bit of an argument before he left this morning, and he went without saying goodbye...'

And he, Jamie, had now to intrude further, unforgiveably, into this privacy of grief with impertinent requests to carry out the final insult on this poor creature's husband. Even talking all clinically and referring to autopsies and legal requirements wasn't going to be much help to him.

God. Who'd be a doctor?

Pre-clinical training had been so simple:

questions and answers, problems and solutions, as cut-and-dried as chess moves. Either you could work out the answer and come up with the diagnosis and cure, or you should not have missed out on so many lectures, and it was time to catch up on some potted-textbook reading. In clinical medicine everything was complicated by the fact that it was *people* you were dealing with, not paper illnesses and academic cures. You could be right all along the line but still lose out; come up with all the right answers but still be left asking the questions. Questions like what to say to this wretched tear-sodden woman in the crumpled blue headscarf whose life had come crashing down about her ears in a short quarter of an hour; questions like why should he, Jamie, helpless spectator as he was, feel, against all logic, as if he was in some way responsible for the calamity?

Sister put an end to his ineffectual stammerings by coming into the room to take over consoling the stricken wife—a task for which even the rawest nurse seemed to have more of an instinct than the most experienced houseman—dismissing him with the curt information that there was an attempted suicide on the way needing his attention.

Great, he thought. Half the population doesn't want to die but I can't do anything to help stop them; now we have the ones who do want to and I've got to do my darnedest to prevent it. This is a mug's game if ever there was one.

She was a student, about nineteen, evidently under enormous pressure with exams looming and boy-friend trouble. Sleeping tablets had been only too readily available, and she had downed a bottleful instead of breakfast when the post brought a goodbye letter from the boy-friend. Fortunately her boy-friend had forgotten a couple of textbooks and gone back to the flat, and found her. Now she was nearly comatose, weeping and vomiting. Somehow Jamie found her altogether easier to show sympathy to—this was within the ready grasp of his imagination. Staff nurse and a junior were already on hand with their nasty clanking trolley of jugs and bowls and rubber tubing for the inevitable stomach washout. He watched as they swung into action with all the expertise of a team working in familiar territory, then went to the phone.

Casualty sister came into the office a moment later, and he put his hand over the receiver.

'You'll be glad to hear that this patient I *am* sending to Intensive Care,' he said. 'Strict observation. She'll be all right. With luck we've caught her early enough, but we can't be too careful. Can we?'

She glared at him. Quite understandable Bob Scrivens not getting far with the chatting up. Jamie tried to imagine her in her karate rig and black belt throwing a line of over-familiar medics over her slim shoulders. What was she like between the sheets? he wondered. Could athleticism be equated with eroticism? Was it worth a few bruises to find out? Judging by their working relationship he wouldn't stand an earthly, but you could never tell—

'Hallo, ICU, Dr McTweed. I'm admitting a barbiturates overdose. She's in Cas. now having a stomach lavage. She'll be with you in half an hour to an hour.' Instructions, details, the feeling that they, highly experienced as they were, probably knew more about it than he did. He would have to go up there later on, of course, and be seen to fulfil his supervisory capacity. He hated the Intensive Care Unit. More machinery than staff, and the girls more like mechanics than nurses. The staff nurse took more pride in being able to make the cardiac monitors behave themselves properly than in keeping the patients comfortable. She even carried a clip-on screwdriver in her top pocket along with her fob watch and pupil torch.

The high-pitched, insistent note of his bleep called him to the telephone and then along to the ward. One of the two or three diabetic patients currently in for stabilization was showing signs of hypoglycaemia, and while the nurses were quite capable of taking the immediate steps necessary and had everything well under control, he was needed to do some re-calculation of the insulin dosages...and of course once he was there, there just happened to be a dozen or so little tasks waiting like forms to fill in, path. slips to check, letters to sign and drugs to write up.'

Then, thankful for the chance of a few minutes' peace, he headed for the canteen and a strong reviving cup of coffee.

He nearly missed seeing Mousie Miniver, who was sitting quietly over in a corner away from the door and the counter, a cup of coffee in front of her on the table, and a copy of *The Nursing Times* lying half-read on her lap. He was tempted to ignore her. He was not in the mood for company, and certainly not for hers. Then some of his anger from the other evening began to rekindle, along with the fresh resolve that had accompanied it.

He went over to her table.

'Can I join you?' he asked. 'I promise not to spill anything down you this time.'

She moved her journal to make room for him but did not say anything.

He sat down in silence. After a while, he said:

'You didn't turn up.'

'No. I...I'm sorry.' She seemed rather flustered, which irritated him. He felt an urge to take her by the shoulders and shake her hard. Instead, he asked in a level tone:

'Why didn't you turn up? You know what we arranged. I waited for you.'

'Yes. Like I said, I'm sorry.'

'Yes, but what happened?'

'I...I thought you were teasing me.'

'What on earth do you mean?'

'Well, you usually take all the dishy girls out; I've seen you. The ones with smashing clothes and loads of self-confidence. Everyone knows they're the sort you go for. I'm not a bit like that, and I don't go out very much, and when you asked me, well, I...I thought it was probably all a bit

166

of a leg-pull.'

Jamie found himself almost won over by the directness and lack of self-pity with which she spoke. He had to take a grip on himself or he would have started sympathizing with the kid, and then where would he have been.

'As if I'd do a thing like that,' he said.

'I know,' she said. 'It was a rotten thing to think, and I'm sorry.'

'What about tonight?'

She hesitated. 'All right,' she said at last.

He finished his coffee, got up to leave, and his white coat caught the edge of her copy of *The Nursing Times*, knocking it to the floor.

'Sorry,' he said, stooping down to retrieve it.

'Don't worry,' she said, simultaneously, leaning across from her chair to pick it up. Their heads met with a resounding knock that could be heard across the canteen.

'Ouch,' said Shirley, straightening up and holding her head ruefully. 'Are you all right?'

Jamie somehow squashed the swearwords which rose to his lips as readily as bubbles in cider, managed a wan grin and forced out some good-natured remark about housemen being a hard-headed lot. *The Nursing Times* lay forgotten on the floor.

She did turn up. And on time, to give her her due. She wore some sort of rather shapeless dress, knitted perhaps—Jamie was not observant about such things—in a sort of knobbly pattern with a lot of red in it. The lipstick she wore matched the colour well enough, but was a hard, rather dark shade which made her skin look whiter and pastier than it needed, a little like a clown's make-up but without the eyebrows and scarlet nose. The scraped-back hair, a plain grey coat and shoulder-bag all conspired to make Jamie think of old photographs he had seen of girls in wartime, struggling with clothes coupons, off to work in munitions factories.

'Hallo,' he said bravely. 'You look nice.'

They did not call him Casanova McTweed for nothing. Actually they did not call him Casanova McTweed at all. But they soon would, he told himself, they soon would.

He took her arm to cross the road to the cinema, a quite acceptable gesture of courtesy and a useful solution to the problem of how first to make actual physical contact, other than knocking heads together. If his hand stayed under her elbow longer than was strictly necessary she did not seem to notice.

He could not have told you afterwards what the film was called. It was some nonsense, in full glorious and glaring colour, about a woman missionary in Africa, a handsome game warden with a band of leopard-skin round his khaki hat, and a whole lot of wild animals, most of which, particularly the baby ones, Mousie obviously, predictably, adored. Probably her maternal instinct. Not a murder in sight. Not even a decent car chase to ease the monotony, let alone a tantalizing glimpse of Susannah York's black suspenders. The little packet of chocolate peanuts which was all he could afford was finished before half-way through the film. He sat there shifting to keep pins and needles at bay, wondering whether he ought to run a BMR test on old Mr Jolly, when he would have to do the marrow biopsy on that young lad with leukaemia who would not like the idea one little bit, and who could blame him?; whether that insulin dosage would prove to be high enough, or whether perhaps they should alter the type he was on...anything in fact to keep from thinking of the warm good-natured group that would even now be assembling in that favourite corner of the White Rabbit bar to unite in drowning memories of the general awfulness of the day.

The climax of the film came with the heroine trying to feed a tiger cub from a baby's bottle (did women missionaries in the wilds of Africa always carry baby's bottles about in their kitbags along with the Good Book and, apparently, a set of hair rollers? Jamie wondered), while the hero with the leopardskin hatband was out with his twelve-bore trying to finish off the cub's mother who was reportedly lying out in the bush grievously wounded by the baddies on safari after pelts. In reality she was only tickled up by a stray bullet and was closing in on the camp, furious, to rescue her young from captivity. As the bushes round the camp rustled ominously and the first growl promised blood to come, Mousie unconsciously clutched at his arm. He looked across at her by the light reflected from the screen. She was totally absorbed, her mouth slightly parted as if in expectation of a kiss. Not a bad profile, really. In fact, from just that angle, in just that light, a disturbingly erotic profile.

Jamie looked away at the screen. When he looked at her face again, only a few seconds later, she had moved. A trick of the light obviously. They'd just be setting up the second round at the White Rabbbit now. Pints too. None of your half-pint nonsense.

He put his other hand lightly on the hand that was clutching his sleeve. She did not notice.

The tiger padded forward towards the heroine's tent. He squeezed the hand and stayed holding it. The tiger leaped, in a glory of gold and tawny and black. Mousie drew her breath in a sharp gasp of terror. He quickly put a protective arm round her shoulders to reassure her. Still no resistance.

Of course the tiger did not even eat the silly girl after all that. It turned out to be an old friend of the game warden's, reared from a cub itself by him (do any of the tigers in Africa manage to reach maturity without the benefit of baby's bottles and interfering humans? Jamie wondered tetchily, pins and needles turning to cramp) and as tame as a lap dog once its own cub was restored and the warden had talked the heroine through her precarious retreat to safety.

Load of old tripe, thought Jamie. Typical woman's film. Trust *her* to enjoy it.

The lights went up. Mousie came back to England, the present time and reality, with an almost audible bump, and with a polite smile exricated herself gently from his en-circling arm.

'Would you like a coffee?' he asked her when they were outside and away from the milling crowd. 'Or something a bit stronger?' There was no harm in trying. Certainly not the White Rabbit, but there were plenty of similar hostelries dotted round Titchford.

To tell the truth, she did fancy something stronger—a gin and tonic, for instance, and not too much tonic. Then she thought of that rather meagre bag of sweets and the way he had gone for the less-expensive seats in the cinema. And how housemen were notorious-ly always broke.

'A coffee would be lovely,' she said, and his heart sank.

He took her to the coffee bar or disco or whatever it called itself near St Mark's Col-lege, the one draped round with nets and fisherman's floats, and huge pink shells like sections of resected intestine. They called the place Davy Jones's Locker and had all sorts of weird and wonderful lighting and sound effects to suggest the bottom of the sea. It was quite an original idea, he conceded, for a place that served nothing more gutsy than the occasional low-calorie shandy. Mousie seemed to like it anyway, or perhaps she was just one of those easy-going people who seemed to like anything. As far as he was concerned, when he was a student the chief pathologist at the hospital had been a singularly oily type of Welshman named Davyd Jones. It had not taken a particularly inventive wit to name the big refrigerated drawers in the mortuary Davy Jones's lockers, and the idea of a place of entertainment similarly named did not appeal to him overmuch. Hardly a promising gambit for chatting up prospective seduction victims, either.

He forced a smile at Mousie across the brown sugar and asked if she had enjoyed the film.

'Oh, yes, I did,' she said warmly. 'I love animals—I often think they're so much nicer than humans, don't you?'

'Yes, I suppose I do, though I'd never really thought about it before. Certainly as a kid I always preferred my hamster to any of the family, even though he bit like anything.'

'I had a white rabbit' (Jamie winced). 'It never bit anyone, I don't think, but it would keep escaping all the time and eating the wrong things in the vegetable garden. Never just grass like any sensible animal that knew its place. It always made a beeline straight for the best lettuce or carrots or whatever was the pride of the moment and the apple of my father's eye. It had an uncanny instinct in that way. Lucky it didn't end up in the cooking-pot the way it used to tempt fate, daft little creature.'

'Was your father a very keen gardener?'

'Oh yes. Still is. My mother always says he has just three interests in life: the church, of course, because he's a clergyman, his garden and his motor-bike. And she teases him that you can't always be sure which order they come in.'

'A parson with a motor-bike sounds unusual.'

'Yes, I suppose it is, really. He has one of those parishes which was originally three or four smaller parishes scattered over the countryside, so places are miles apart and he has an enormous amount of travelling to do. I used to ride pillion with him when I was a kid. I'd just cling on and close my eyes tight. I never dared admit he scared the life out of me. I don't think anyone knew that except my brother.'

'At least you got some sympathy then?'

'Yes, in a way. Sympathetic teasing I suppose it was. He gave me this, but I think he meant it more as a joke.' She pulled out a little St Christopher medallion the size of an old sixpence which hung, along with a tiny silver cross, on a chain under the high neck of her dress.

'But, joke or not, you wear it.'

'Yes. Perhaps he should have given Daddy one as well. It wasn't just a matter of nerves, you know. Parson or not, he's quite the most dangerous driver around our area. It's a standing joke in the village, stay indoors when Parson Miniver's out on his motor-bike. Mum and I are always trying to per-suade him to get a little car which might be a bit safer. But he just says there'll be time enough for playing the old man when he's retired.'

'My dad's the exact opposite. He's a surgeon, rather a good one actually...'

'I know,' said Mousie.

'...and he has a horror of doing anything that could harm his hands. Like having a road accident, for instance. So he's the safest driver imaginable, which is rather a pity because he buys quite exciting cars, then doesn't come anywhere near to doing them justice.'

But Jamie's mind was not really on the conversation, or the relative attitudes to driving of their respective fathers. He was wondering whether he would be push-ing his luck to let their hands touch accidentally-on-purpose yet again, and how long he dared leave his hand there next time, how soon he could take her back to the nurses' home and combine the maximum evening's progress with the maximum night's sleep. He was also remembering and running over in his mind the long-neglected details of the art of the pavement good night.

He acquitted himself well, he decided, looking back later. Gentle enough not to scare her away, masterly enough to impress her and keep a firm hold on the initiative in their relationship. The main trouble with taking it all so slowly and circumspectly was the danger of getting to know the kid, even to like her.

Oh no, what was he thinking of; there was precious little likelihood of that! What him—Jamie McTweed—get friendly with a parson's daughter? Pull the other leg! He'd made a resolution, he was *quite* up to sticking to it.

For all his progress and his determination on that particular front he was not best pleased to have a late-night visitor, in the form of Bob Scrivens with some corny just-happened-to-be-passing routine, who invited himself in, ignoring the fact that Jamie was in pyjamas and obviously on his way to a relatively early night. He plonked a couple of cans of beer down on the table and himself down in the only armchair with his feet slung sideways over the arms, and said:

'All alone in your own little bed then? You do disappoint me.'

Jamie tugged viciously at the ring-pull of one of the beer cans, to be rewarded with a violent spray of at least half the contents over a fair part of the room and a square yard of the ceiling.

'Hey, gently now.' Bob made a poor attempt at concealing his amusement.

'Damn the thing! What did you do to it?'

'Me? I only ran up the stairs two at a time with a can in each pocket, in my eagerness to see you.'

Jamie mopped angrily. Bob pulled the other ring with considerable circumspection and smugly avoided the same disaster. Jamie did not offer to find him a glass.

'I'm surprised you haven't come calling for your thirty quid yet. Or is it a matter of paying me mine?' said Bob.

'No, it certainly isn't. Just give me time. Rome wasn't built in a day.'

Bob shrugged. 'OK, so how are you getting on with that Sabine woman?'

'Well enough. We went to the cinema this evening.'

'Oh, big deal!' said Bob sarcastically. 'The great lover! You'll be telling me next you actually shared the same bag of crisps in the back row.'

'These things need tact and charm. *You* wouldn't know about that. Some girls can't just be met, bought one drink and yanked into bed.'

'If you say so,' said Bob sceptically. 'If you ask me, they all respond to the caveman approach.'

'Well, all I can say is, if you've never met one who didn't, perhaps that's your loss.'

Bob took a long pull of his beer and belched appreciatively.

'Well,' he said, 'don't take too long about it. You know where to find me. And I'd rather not risk a cheque if you don't mind.'

CHAPTER EIGHT

For Carrie Masterson nursing was proving rather less glamorous and a good deal harder work than she had ever in her idealistic schooldays imagined. For one thing, her idea had usually been of men patients, mostly young, mostly handsome, all decidedly grateful for the least little thing she and her fellow labourers could do—aided in their untiring efforts of course by young, handsome doctors with flashing smiles who were equally impressed by their every effort.

And instead here she was, stuck on Women's Surgical with nasty smelly drainages and dirty dressings, her life ruled by bedpan rounds, no glamour at all to the work, and precious little to the people. She was too tired at the end of a working day to do anything much off duty except kick off her shoes and throw herself down exhausted on the bed; and on duty the only men she saw were porters who were cheeky and over-familiar, or the occasional doctor who shone like a star in her humble sky, an object of awed respect rather than professional comradeship. Dr Doyle, though, *was* rather handsome. He even spoke to her sometimes too, asked her routine questions about the patients' progress. It was all there in the report book in the office, but if for some reason he preferred to ask her rather than go in the office and look, that was up to him, and it made her day. He would ask her to chaperone when he examined patients and of course she did, though even she, new as she was, knew that he should have asked via Sister. What seemed to her unfair, indeed incomprehensible, was that it was she who received the blasting from Sister Blandish that the bedpan round was unfinished because she was chaperoning for an examination of Mrs Dunbar, while Dr Doyle who had given the order received only the most winning of smiles from the old toad for what was blatantly his fault. That, she was rapidly discovering, was the sort of justice one expected working in a hospital. She went about her business with a sigh.

Dr Doyle, meanwhile, stayed to chat to Janet Dunbar.

'The fact is,' he told her, 'you could sit here for ever, drinking as much as possible and hoping to pass the stone spontaneously. But we all know you've got better things to do, so the next thing is to see if we can't give the stone a bit of help.' He fumbled among the X-ray plates. 'Now, while no one is one hundred per cent certain, it seems that this is almost certainly the stone. You can see that in this picture taken a week after this one it appears to have shifted a little bit. So we are going to take you down to the operating theatre and pass a tiny tube into your bladder and up towards the kidney in the hope of getting it out.'

'Sort of lassooing it, do you mean?'

'Something like that.'

'And it usually works, does it?' It sounded a bit scarey to her, though he talked as if it was commonplace. Probably was, to him.

'Let's say it's worth trying.'

'And if it doesn't work?'

'We'll cross that bridge when we come to it, shall we?'

He got his notes together and slid the X-rays back into their envelope, smiled his reassuring smile for Janet's benefit, and threw back the cubicle curtains with a practised swish...almost in the face of an advancing Margaret Llewellyn.

Janet swore silently. Just when she could have done with some peace and quiet to consider this latest development.

'Hallo,' she said, aware with only the slightest sense of guilt that she sounded about as unwelcoming as she felt.

But Margaret Llewellyn, daunting today in a hat that was reminiscent of nothing so much as a funeral wreath with only the white card missing, seemed more interested in Bill Doyle than in Janet herself.

'Wait, young man,' she commanded, grabbing him by the white coat with the tenacity of a police dog making an arrest before he could walk away. 'I know your mother,' she said, which was evidently meant to explain such an odd action.

Janet, with a horrified sense of déjà-vu, watched as she marched him to the side of the ward, just by the empty bed between her and the gall bladder with the blue nightie. Tall young man bent slightly to listen to plump officious woman. Eyes round the ward watched. This odd, objectionable friend of Janet Dunbar's was one of the few current diversions in life and they were not going to miss anything if they could help it.

They saw him straighten up with surprise at something she said, heard her silence his exclamations of surprise and protest with a firm, 'Never mind how I know. Just listen to what I have to say,' then go on more quietly as if trying to persuade him of something. They heard her say: 'Only on that condition, mind.' And when Bill Doyle smiled, as if agreeing to whatever it was, and then ask a question, they heard, not for the first time: 'Quite easily. Miss Gray's not a close friend of mine for nothing, you know.' And they saw him take a white envelope from her with reluctant gratitude.

Janet questioned her, of course, but got only a Mysterious Look, which was not one of her more endearing expressions.

After she had gone, the subsequent concurrence of public opinion among the other patients was that she was bribing him in some way, probably to facilitate Janet's transfer to bigger and better things in the grandeur of a side ward or even the private wing. It did not make Janet's life among her fellows any more comfortable despite her protests that she had no idea what the conversation was about and would not in any case want to move away from their company.

Janet herself was more inclined to assume

that somebody's private life was being busy-bodied with, and though she felt she would really rather not know the details, it left her feeling vaguely uncomfortable.

Typically, Angus came to her rescue with his earthy reassurance.

'It was probably some message from the boy's mother. She keeps going on about knowing her, and the size of telephone bills that woman must run up in a quarter would daunt a millionaire. Perhaps for once she's economizing. Anyway, it's no business of ours, so stop thinking about it.'

Staff Nurse Miniver walked past, a kidney dish with cotton-wool swab and used syringe in her hand, having surprised some apprehensive patient with the painlessness of her injection giving, on her way to the clinical room.

'All right, Mrs Dunbar? No pain?'

'No, I'm fine at the moment, thanks.'

'It's good news that they're doing something about you at last. It'll make a change from lying there drinking lemonade all day, won't it?'

She looked more cheerful than usual, thought Janet. Not that she was usually a misery or anything like that, just that she semed more cheerful nowadays.

'That's the one I was telling you about.' She nudged Angus. 'The one who's always so kind and thoughtful.'

'Well, I should think once you're out of here you'd better invite her over to see us. She looks as if she could do with a bit of your home cooking to fatten her up,' commented Angus. 'The poor lass is nothing but skin and bone.'

Jamie McTweed did not intentionally let two or three days go by before seeing Mousie Miniver again. The way things were going he was determined to press home his advantage as soon as possible, get his hands on the money of Bob's and forget the whole incident. But those two days on take were unusually punishing. The nurse-mechanics of the ICU would never, it seemed, get the idea of clearing the beds as much as possible before the weekend, when a high percentage of Titchford's middle-aged athletically ambitious citizens left their sedentary office jobs and went at their gardens, allotments or, more recently, their jogging, like bulls at a gate, unaware that their poor coronary systems simply were not in a fit state to cope. If Jamie, a comparative newcomer to the game, could see the predictability of the pattern, and expect at least three or four coronaries each weekend, why could ICU Sister not do the same, and be prepared? Every weekend she bleated that her beds were full, that she had insufficient staff to cope and (best of all) why had she not been warned? It was all, needless to say, the direct fault of the duty admitting officer, and Jamie had by now learned to keep his mouth shut under this added insult rather than make things worse by putting the record straight. The result was the last-minute shuffling of some of the slightly-improved cases out to the general wards (who in turn grumbled that this had been left to the weekend) in order to empty ICU beds. The other alternative was the admission of seriously ill patients direct to general wards where the staff were not always in a position to cope adequately, nor, by the general nature of the new system really expected to. Medicine was supposed to be Jamie's job, not public-relations expert and playing United Nations peacemaking force to a group of menopausal nursing sisters who couldn't get themselves properly organized.

One way and another, by the time he eventually had some time to call his own, Jamie realized that he had been on his feet almost non-stop through nearly nine changes of nursing shift and that most of the hospital had enjoyed about ten times as much sleep as he had in the course of the preceding two days. So that when he next saw Mousie he was not exactly looking his debonair best. In fact he nearly knocked the girl down as he staggered bleary-eyed away from the general direction of Casualty just as she, fresh-looking as ever, came along the main corridor.

The weary greeted the timid.

Yes, it seemed she was free that evening.

'Good. What about—' A poster above her head advertised a recital to be given by a local string quartet in one of the Titchford churches. Sounded deadly. But the date was right. So was the price—FREE, in large letters. Even if they pushed a plate under people's noses it would be cheaper than the flicks. 'What about a concert? Do you like music?'

The idea evidently quite impressed her, and he notched himself up a mental good mark for brilliant extemporization. They arranged where to meet. He found his eyes wandering to the neck of her rather plain blouse, but only a glimpse of chain at the back of her neck was visible. It was somehow tantalizing that even this modest piece of personal adornment was not on full show.

He went back to his room, had a bath and a shave and felt better. A concert in a church was a double stroke of genius, it suddenly occurred to him, as no girl could expect to be regaled with eatables during the music as if it was a film. That was not overdoing the meanness even for a Scotsman—Mousie had never *expected* anything, unlike the vultures he usually took around. And just because of it...where was that little box of fruit jellies that Awful Great Aunt Maud had so unsuitably produced for his last birthday? Down among the clean shirts somewhere. He would give them to Mousie; such an old-fashioned gesture would appeal to a girl like that.

It did. Her whole face lit up in a rather appealing way he had not noticed before.

They found two places among the audience in the hard wooden pews, and soon the players sat down with much scraping of chairs and adjusting of music stands. They scratched away for a few minutes, tuning up, Jamie supposed, though it did not sound much different to him when the programme proper started. He watched her reading studiously through the closely-typed notes on the mimeographed sheet, then turn her full concentration to the music. He remembered no more, not another note, until Mousie nudged him awake at the end.

'I didn't think it would look very good if you snored through the vicar's closing prayer,' she said, laughing, once they were safely outside.

Genuinely ashamed, he made the most convincing apologetic noises he could muster. *This* was not doing very much for his Great Lover image at all. Shirley, however, far from being offended or seeing it as any sort of personal affront, was all sympathy.

'I know how hard you have to work, Jamie. If I had had any consideration I should have said No when you suggested this evening, so if it's anyone's fault it's mine. Please don't worry. Actually, I thought it was rather funny, those poor musicians throwing themselves body and soul into their performance while you sat in your quiet corner completely dead to the world. I don't think anyone noticed, anyway. You still look pretty exhausted to me. It's rotten the way they treat you. There's only one place you should be this evening, you know, and that's in bed.'

There just had to be an answer to that, but Jamie carefully restrained himself. This was not Selina or Staff Nurse Mackie he was dealing with.

Without either of them being aware of it, a new easiness had crept into their relationship, an element of fellow-feeling as if they were not on separate sides of their own private battle (as in Jamie's mind) but more united on the same side against the awfulness of Them, the mighty machine, the hospital authorities. It was not a development that Jamie would have chosen, but now he would just have to make the best use he could of it.

They went for the quickest of coffees, she insisting in an almost motherly way that he must get an early night, then walked back along the path round the edge of the park.

He took her hand and she squeezed his fingers gently. He kissed her in the shadows inside the park gates. Their first kiss a few days earlier had been awkward and uncertain, noses getting the wrong way round to each other, apologies and shy laughter. This time she was half expecting it, perhaps even half hoping he told himself, and it was a far less unfortunate (if still not, on his part at least, a particularly enjoyable) experience.

'You're very quiet,' she said as they walked on their way again, his arm round her waist. A trained actress could not have delivered him his cue with better timing.

'I was just thinking how dreadful it was of me to behave so badly this evening. I don't know how I can make it up to you.' She was obviously going to protest, so he hurried on before she could say anything: 'I was wondering...well' (half hesitant now, as if the idea has just come to you, not as if it is all a game of spider and fly) '...I suppose you wouldn't like to come round to my place, on Saturday evening say...'

He half expected signs of alarm from Mousie; she showed none, so the big hungry cat took another step or so closer.

'I'm not much of a cook,' he went on humbly, 'but I can manage a steak and we could have a bottle of wine and listen to some of my old Beatles records...'

Most girls, most Titchford girls, particularly most St Lawrence's girls, however green, would have been wary of an invitation like that. But she accepted unquestioningly. She even seemed quite keen on the idea.

And he, unscrupulous scoundrel that he was, was all set to take full advantage of her trust and innocence.

'I gather it didn't work, then,' said Janet Dunbar.

'No, I'm afraid not. I'm sorry.'

'It's not your fault, Nurse Miniver. That's one thing I can be sure of.'

'No, but it's wretched for you.'

'Yes, the pain's as bad now as it ever was.

Is it possible they actually moved the stone a little bit, not enough to get it out as they planned, but enough...eeekk...to set this pain off again?'

A cool reassuring hand against hers.

'The injection will work in a few minutes. Try to lie still. Yes, it's possible that's what happened. Or that it just started up spontaneously again.'

'And now they're going to operate, properly. To cut it out, I mean.'

'Yes. Tomorrow. They're afraid from the X-ray evidence that it may be beginning to damage the tissues and they can't risk that. It'll be all right, there's no need to be apprehensive. You'll be starved from midnight tonight—'

'Ugh,' Janet was feeling the pain a bit less already, and prepared to risk a feeble joke, 'the hospital's economizing again, is it?'

'That's right. You'll probably be fairly early on the list and they'll give you a pre-med injection that'll make you feel all pleasant and drowsy and a bit dry in the mouth, and change you into these silly clothes they insist on, and off you'll go. This afternoon the physio will come and have a chat and go through various breathing exercises and things they'll want you to do when you come round from the anaesthetic. And now I would like you to sign this consent form agreeing to have the operation done.'

'Anything to get this trouble cleared up, and have an end to this pain. D'you know, I'd forgotten just how bad it could be. I suppose it's like having a baby, you tend to forget the bad parts when they are not actually happening to you.'

'That's right. Now read it carefully before you sign. Yes, just there, please.'

Well, thought Janet, the pethidine bringing its familiar haziness once again, she had been through the cystoscopy or whatever they called it. She might as well be hanged for a sheep as a lamb. What was the point in consulting Angus before she signed? It was her pain, and anything that got rid of it would be welcome...

'How's my favourite staff nurse then?' asked Jamie McTweed.

'Indulging in her usual hatred of diabetics,' said Staff Nurse Mackie. 'Don't just stand there like a helpless male, come and help me check this wretched insulin.'

Jamie took the opportunity of kissing the fluffy little bits of hair at the back of her neck, a part of female anatomy he found, without exception, quite irresistible.

'Don't be cheeky,' said Mackie unenthusiastically.

'You nurses been paid yet? We've another week to go.'

'Why, are you planning to marry me for my money?'

'Not if I can get it without.'

'Charming!'

'But frank. You must admit that.'

That neck, delectable as it was, was missing something. What was it? He could not think.

'Look...are you watching?' She had the insulin bottle upside down on the needle and was drawing up the fluid into the syringe. 'There, now is that right?'

'How much should it be?'

'Chart's on the table. You wrote it, for goodness sake.'

'I've written up drugs for some fifty patients one way and another during the past 24 hours. Let's see. Yes, that's right. We'll see if the different sort of insulin suits him better. Don't go for a minute—'

The little rounded white collar of the dress, the pearl stud-button, the pale skin, definitely an area of delight on any girl, so what was needed. Something, for sure. Perhaps...could it be that she lacked just a glimpse of thin, silver chain among the soft down?'

'Don't tell me, let me guess. You want a sub again.'

'Just a couple of quid. For a few days.'

'You haven't paid me back that last quid yet.'

'I will, you'll see. You shall have it all together.'

'Promises, promises.'

'It's urgent, Mackie.'

'Oh, yes,' she mocked. 'Well, we all know what that means.'

'Oh?'

'The steak and bottle of wine routine. "I am not much of a cook but we can listen to my old Bing Crosby records." You're not very original, are you, Jamie? Who's the lucky victim this time, then? Selina again?'

'None of your business.'

'Not even if I'm supposed to subsidize the exercise?'

'No. And stop jumping to conclusions. Just be a sport and lend me the money.'

'It's the last time, mind. Positively the last.'

'Promise.' When this was all over, Mackie must be seriously cultivated. She was a tower of strength. 'Bless you, kid-o.'

'It's pounds, not dollars, you know,' said Mackie drily.

CHAPTER NINE

If he said it himself, thought Jamie, he should have been a stage manager. By the time Saturday evening came his little bachelor pad looked as romantic as any theatrical set.

By dint of an extra couple of hours worked for someone here, a neat bit of doubling up there, a corner or two of the ward work if not cut then distinctly trimmed with the connivance of Mackie and a blind eye from Sister Elliott (though, since she was afflicted by a glide in her eyes anyway, it would have been difficult to tell which was supposed to be the blind one she turned); fingers crossed that nothing major erupted at the last moment...and bingo, he managed to get from mid-Saturday afternoon onwards to himself.

The place was clean. That was a start. Some old duck in a huge flowered pinny that seemed to go round even her vast form at least twice before it tied, and with a perpetual cigarette attached as if by glue to her bottom lip, was supposed to come and shake a mop at it every Friday. Jamie hardly ever saw her but he knew when she had been there because the flat smelt of her cigarette instead of stale beer and cooking, and if he remembered to move the ash off the furniture and did not actually make any fresh mess the place was still presentable on Saturday.

He sometimes liked to exalt the place by calling it a flat. The hospital authorities, who had it on a long lease as accommodation for whoever held his job, as there was not enough room in the hospital residence, were pleased to call it a flat, so why shouldn't he? In fact it was a bedsitter plain and simple. One bed, one table, one easy chair, one hard chair. Come to think of it, only a chamber pot and Bible were missing to complete the illusion that his present existence was a prison sentence.

He put the lettuce to soak in the wash basin, perched the long French loaf on top of the books in the bookshelf out of the way and sat the steak in its plastic bag on his one chipped tin plate on the top of the tiny cooker in the alcove. There was a cloth for the table in the back of the drawer where the cutlery lived. It could have done with an iron over it, but a good shake would have to do. What did she think this place was anyway?—the Ritz? Next he found the old straw-covered Chianti bottle left behind under the washbasin by the previous tenant, and poked around to find the candle he knew was lurking between the tin of chicken curry and the packet of over-sweet drinking chocolate on the shelf below the socks and clean handkerchiefs drawer. The candle would not fit in the top of the bottle. Shave a bit off with one of the steak knives. That's better, except there were shavings of grease on the carpet.

Knife, fork, side plate. No butter, could not run to that. Have to make do with the soft stuff in one of those flowery tubs, probably better for them anyway—a good talking point if the evening was so grim they ended up talking shop all the time. The role of polysaturated fats in arterio-sclerotic pathology. Great stuff.

He put the cover over the bed and search-ed round for the matching covers that fit-ted the pillows, supposedly turning them into cushions and the bed into a settee for daytime. Not that anyone was ever fooled. Not even Mousie presumably, but the effort was obviously necessary. (The bed would, he trusted, come into its own later on anyway.)

Just the final touch was missing now. He left the door on the latch and went down-stairs to the basement flat. Mrs Francis, the caretaker, and the smell of onions frying reached the door simultaneously. Mrs Fran-cis was small and weasly-looking with a small weasly-looking child of indeterminate sex and a large weasly-looking cat. Along with the smell of onions was the hint of a whiff in the air suggesting that one or other (or both) of the latter could have been more perfectly house-trained. Although hardened to most of the smells of the hospital, Jamie found it difficult to hide his distaste at this particular olfactory assault; but he quickly turned on the charming far-from-home-please-mother-me attitude which he had learned worked wonders with Mrs Francis.

'Hallo, dear. D'yer want a cup of tea? Come in. There's always some in the pot.'

Jamie went in but funked the cup of tea.

'I wondered if you had any coins for the meter, Mrs F? I'm right out.'

'Shouldn't really, dearie. Yer know the rules. Still, since it's you...' She went off to search for her purse.

Mrs Francis's great talent in life was growing things. Pots of flowers, alive, dead, recuperating, took pride of place on every ledge and shelf, and a colourful window-box blocked the light from the open window. Jamie backed nonchalantly towards it. The child watched him sullenly, thumb stuck firmly in its weasly face.

'Just this once, mind,' she bustled back. 'What if everyone came knocking?' She counted the coins into his outstretched hand and took his fifty-pence piece.

'I'm not everyone, Mrs F. Thanks again.' he blew her a cheeky kiss from the door.

The hand behind his back yielded a couple of daffodils, an anemone bud and half a dozen assorted leaves. In that little potted-meat jar they did not look bad on the table. Not bad at all.

He washed and shaved, leering in the little mirror over the basin and making Handsome Brute faces at himself, then splashed on a generous amount of the after-shave an aunt who took television advertisements at face value had decided was just the thing up-and-coming young medical men should be splashing themselves with. Little did she know, he thought. Next a white roll-neck sweater under a darkish jacket, casual but with a hint of sophistication. Should have been a velvet smoking jacket really, proper seducer's uniform—a touch of the Noel Cowards. But he had not got one anyway. And it would not do to over-act and spoil everything.

A last-minute touch of brilliance for the table, he remembered that little bottle of French dressing in the cupboard left from the days when that funny plump little staff nurse on the orthopaedic theatre had taken it upon herself to try and waft a breath of civilization into his uncouth existence—a pleasant enough process of introducing glasses to replace a shared toothmug for drinking out of, a Boots reproduction picture on the wall to replace a succession of more or less randy posters, a tasteful ornament or so on the window sill. Come to think of it, that was probably where the tablecloth originated from. Not bad times, those, until it became evident just how far the takeover was planned to go.

He shook the dressing vigorously then splashed a liberal amount over the green salad. She might not like it, but at least they would both have the same amount of garlic on their breaths. (Where had he heard that garlic was supposed to be an aphrodisiac? Oh, well, you never knew your luck.)

He looked at his watch. She should be here soon. He opened the wine bottle and poured himself a glass. Flying speed, as his old man would call it. He was enjoying this evening, he realized. It had enough of an element of the hunt to set his adrenalin running, enough certainty of a satisfactory outcome to allow him to relax and savour the chase. He could not pretend it was the first time his little lair had seen such assignments, but this one had the added undertones of the wager nearly won and he basked in a tingle of predatory excitement at the prospect.

She was a few minutes late and apologized. She wore a powder blue dress with a loopy sort of ornamental work round the collar and some beads, long but knotted at about throat level. She had some quite pretty pearl ear-rings on but they did not quite match the beads. For some reason it irritated him that she did not make the best of what assets she had. After all every girl must have *some* assets, just being feminine insured that.

'Hallo,' he said, setting out determinedly to be totally charming. He knew he ought to say something about how nice she looked, but this time every instinct baulked at such perjury. But he did manage: 'Mmm, you smell good, and that at least was true. She had on a strong, but not too strong, perfume, light and flowery—yet not just a straight smell of some single recognizable flower, rather a mixture of flowers, or flowers and Something which he could not define but which in a tantalizing and intangible way reminded him of something or some time in his life, perhaps as a child, that was totally happy.

'What would you like to drink?' he asked. 'I've got a splendid choice: wine, wine or, er, wine.'

She laughed. 'I suppose you haven't any wine, have you?'

'There now, it just so happens you're in luck. Cheers.'

She walked round the little room, glass in hand, looking at the books in his shelves and on the table between the foot of his bed-settee and the window, medical textbooks mostly, a few science-fiction, a couple of paperback thrillers.

'You ought to meet my brother,' she said. 'He's a science-fiction fanatic, so you'd have a taste in common. He reads all these stories avidly but he keeps saying. "Can't you see, that wouldn't happen because such-and-such a formula wouldn't work like they say it would, or the man-eating plant in chapter two should have been poisoned by using something or other before it got out of hand," and he pulls the whole plot to pieces. I don't really know why he bothers to read them, when you think about it. Are you like that?'

'No. When I do have time to read I just

like a good yarn. I'm not worried if the details don't hang together. I'm not really very scientifically minded anyway.'

'That's surprising, isn't it? With you being a doctor?'

'I don't think so. Doctors aren't really primarily scientists, after all. Any more than nurses are.'

She paused to peer at the cluster of very amateur family snapshots on the mantel-piece. He expected to be required to identify places and people. Instead she straightened up. 'I like the picture,' she said. 'It makes a change from the posters people usually seem to have on their walls. It's a famous one, isn't it? I'm sure I've seen it somewhere before.'

He had to admit he did not know. He took care not to add that he didn't much care, that it was only there because the plump staff nurse had put it there and becaue it hid a rather ugly damp mark on the wall.

'Have some more wine,' he said, topping her glass right up and hoping she did not know the song about Having Some Madeira, M'dear.

'Where would you like to sit? Not much of a choice, I'm afraid.'

She chose the bed, then leant forward to look at the pile of records that had caught her eye; she slid forward until she was kneeling on the carpet, and picked up one or two to inspect. She had an unconscious gesture of rubbing her cheek with her fingertips when she was concentrating on something. He joined her on the carpet, and their heads came interestingly close as they looked together at the printing on the record sleeves.

' "Penny Lane", that's one of my favourites,' she said. 'Do you know before I first heard it I always thought it was a girl's name, and the song was all about her.'

'What are your other favourites; I'll see if I've got them.'

'Oh, "Eleanor Rigby", I think. It's so true and so sad. "All the lonely people, where do they all belong?" It nearly makes me cry sometimes.'

'Well, we want something a bit more cheerful now, don't you think?' Jamie steered the conversation very determinedly. 'What about "She loves you, yeah, yeah, yeah..."? '

'Fine.'

He put the record on, then rolled up his sleeves with what he hoped looked like panache ready to cook the steak.

'Can I help?' Since he had realized that it is a bit difficult to play the role of suave seducer convincingly when one has forgotten to peel the mushrooms, he reluctantly thrust the basket towards her and rooted out an old newspaper for the bits.

While the steak sizzled and spat appetizingly in the pan Jamie lit the candle in the chianti bottle. The cutlery, collected piece by piece with the labels from breakfast-cereal packets, glittered rewardingly. Almost like silver. He replaced an ebullient John, Paul, George and Ringo with "Songs for Soft-hearted Sweethearts" turned down low. All très romantic, he congratulated himself.

The steak was a bit burnt, the salad a bit drab. Mousie said how good the mushrooms were; he pointed out that this was all a matter of how well they had been peeled, and she had already drunk enough to find this a witty compliment.

'Let me fill up your glass,' said Jamie.

She was obviously not very used to alcohol. That was all to the good. She was talking freely, amusingly even. She was a mine of hospital gossip, of fascinating titbits of information that were obviously common knowledge among the nursing staff but many of them new to him, and a far cry from the kiss-and-tell type of gossip of the White Rabbit. She knew too about books, about things like music and poetry—the sort of things that filled the conversation when his parents had dinner parties, and left him wishing he had shown a bit more interest at school—though she was suitably apologetic for her accomplishments when she mistook his admiring silence for boredom. 'The headmistress at my school seemed to think it did you more

216

good in life to be able to spout poems and know a string quartet from a symphony than to be able to do logarithms or pass exams or even win lacrosse matches,' she said.

The romantic atmosphere, which had begun to build up quite well over dinner, was interrupted by the mundane task of clearing the dishes (anyone who knew Jamie would have been immediately suspicious at the fact that he refused to let his visitor wash them up) and not helped by the fact that when Shirley wanted to 'powder her nose' he had to direct her along a cold landing and up a flight of stairs to a dank room that smelt of damp with an antiquated cistern that clanked like some piece of apparatus in a shipyard; and that the automatic landing light ran out of time and clicked itself out, leaving her in pitch blackness half-way down the stairs so that she had to grope her way back to his room, half nervous, half laughing.

While she was out he folded the little table

back against the wall, replaced the now-dying candle with a dim lamp on the bookshelf, turned the gas fire on low and turned the record over to its smoochier side.

She sat down again on one end of the bed. Like a lamb to the slaughter, he thought. This is going to be a push-over. They thought I couldn't do it. Or wouldn't do it. I'll show them I can, and will, get any girl I've a mind to.

'Is that really your father's book?' She indicated a rather battered McTweed on Plastic Surgery on the bottom shelf of the bookshelf (it was too massive to go anywhere else). Jamie would never admit how proud he was of those plump tomes, and made it a perverse point of honour, almost like inverted snobbery, to have a distinctly dog-eared and several-editions-out-of-date copy rather than a pristine up-to-date copy, readily available at home.

'That? Oh...er, yes, it is actually.' He was almost too casual.

'It must be wonderful to know your name

will go on living in something like that even long after you are dead.'

'My father is very far from dead.'

'Oh, I didn't mean that. I'm very glad he is. And it must be marvellous for you—the book and the reflected glory and everything.'

'There isn't much of that really, you know. People just expect me to know the whole book by heart, and to have a natural gift for plastic surgery which is a specialty which bores me anyway.' It was high time they got down to business. 'And we don't want to talk about him and his wretched book. Not at a time like this. What we should be talking about—' he began surreptitiously to manoeuvre along the bed towards her— 'is something far more interesting. You.'

'Me?' She looked a bit surprised. Mustn't rush it at this stage. 'But you know all about me already.'

'Your name, your schooldays, your family, your work, yes. But that's words, all words. It's you I want to know about, not things

219

about you. What are words between people like us, after all? Have you never heard of body language? Do you not realize that your whole body is crying out to me for attention and response? You know this deep in yourself, don't you—every movement you make, every gesture tells me about you and invites me to find out more. Words only hide such things. Each lift of your head, each move of your arm is a crying out for love and appreciation that your lips are afraid to make, that perhaps you are not even fully aware of...'

She was sitting very still, very upright, slightly flushed and breathing rather quickly.

It was a good approach, this. It had never failed yet and it showed no danger of failing now.

'This cheek now, look at it,' he went on, cupping his hand against the warm curve of her skin. 'The sheer sensuousness of it— oh, you women, I sometimes think you have no idea how you torment a man. This fine hair, here, the soft bits at the back of your neck. You've no idea how my fingers have longed to stroke that hair, how I have dreamed of letting my hands rest here, where your skin is soft and white.'

His face was once more within a few inches of hers. She should be feeling his warm, passion-laden breath on her cheek. Should he waste time kissing her to lay a firmer claim to the neckline and all territories north, or keep his hands on the move in shoulderstrap country, maintaining the momentum of the attack but perhaps risking everything by too much haste? Both, he decided. Attack on all fronts; don't give her time to collect herself and realize what you are up to.

The left hand started to stray surreptitiously downwards, gently moving round inside the loose circle of her collar. His lips moved slowly nearer and nearer to hers (she was mesmerized, he could sense it. Trapped like a rabbit in a car's headlights. That was good). His right hand moved across to rest on her thigh, ready to do some exploring on its own account while her attention was occupied elsewhere.

Now was the moment. He would kiss her gently, unassumingly at first, then harder and more passionately, apparently carried away by a pathetic, hungry longing. If this did not appear to be achieving the required response he would have to try putting the pathetic hungry bit into words. A few well chosen poetic phrases with words like Hanker and Yearn and Hopeless Passion and Adore from Afar—guaranteed to arouse whatever instinct in a girl required arousing.

Her face moved fractionally towards his, her eyes closed expectantly, her lips parted slightly ready to be kissed. What was he waiting for? He hardly knew himself, but something was distracting him and putting him right off his stride. Of course. It was those stupid owl-eyed glasses of hers (What was it?—Men never make passes at girls who wear glasses...) They would have to go. Unwilling to sacrifice territory successfully annexed in the skirt region he used the hand currently deployed exploring the neck and shoulders to try to remove the offending monstrosities. One side came free without any trouble. The other side, away from him, was not so successful and, with the glasses now hanging lopsided, the more he struggled the more he succeeded only in entangling the earpiece in her hair. He gave a tug and she winced.

'Here,' she said, 'let me do it.' her hands went up to her head, and the sleeves of her dress fell back from the cuffs showing pale wrists with a fine brown down on them. For a few seconds she fumbled almost as ineffectually as he had done, then she freed the glasses by reaching impatiently behind her head and loosing the clip of the tortoiseshell buckle that held her hair so sternly in check.

The effect was dramatic, and Jamie gasped. For suddenly this thick brown mass of hair came tumbling round her ears and down to her shoulders, in the soft light gleaming and glinting every shade of copper and gold and rich dark chestnut. It made a soft framing halo, and her whole face seemed to come to life. The lines of her features were softer and gentler, her cheeks were plumper, and delicious puckering little dimples awoke near her mouth which, surely, were not there before. Her ears were pale and delicate as shells. Her eyes sparkled.

All unaware, she folded the offending glasses and reached to put them on the bookshelf.

'Let me take them,' he said.

She smiled at him, and it was as if he had never seen her properly until that moment. She was—yes—there was only one way to say it—she was quite simply—*beautiful*.

Completely taken aback, he sat and stared at her, speechless.

'What on earth's the matter, Jamie? What are you looking at me like that for?'

'I'm sorry, I didn't...I mean...why don't you always look like that?' he stammered, feeling rather foolish.

'On duty, you mean?' she laughed. 'Can't you just imagine me going round the ward half blind without my specs, and with my hair falling into all the medicines. That would give Sister Blandish a real field day, to be sure.' He had not even noticed before what a pretty voice she had.

'I just meant...well, with your hair loose... and no glasses...you look so different...so pretty...' Now, when he actually meant the compliment, it sounded clumsy and unconvincing.

He shifted abruptly back along the bed.

'I'll make some coffee,' he said sharply. 'Do you like black or white?'

The pause that followed developed into an awkward silence, harder to break the longer it lasted. Puzzled and upset, each for different reasons, they drank their coffee in silence and looked everywhere except at each other.

The discovery of what she was really like should on the face of it have made his task a whole lot easier. Instead, he knew he could no more go ahead with his Master Plan for the evening now than fly, though the mixture of his own emotions confused him too much to be quite sure why.

When he was a boy he once found a bird's egg lying on the grass under a tree. It was smooth and oval and so perfectly blue that he was enchanted by it. Yet some destructive urge, or perhaps simply curiosity had made him long to break it. Time after time through the day he went back to look at it: perhaps it was not an egg at all, but some sort of semi-precious stone that, miraculously, a blow would not destroy. At last he made his mind up, and broke the egg with a stick. All that was left of his precious, delicate treasure was a mess of crushed shell, slime and orange yolk on the grass. And a terrible sense of loss and shame that made him cry himself to sleep for many nights afterwards.

He remembered it now, almost as if he had only just been stopped short of committing some repeat of his youthful vandalism. He felt excited, too, in an odd way ashamed of himself and—quite illogically—angry.

Blast Mousie Miniver for not being plain

and unimportant and usable!

Blast Bob Scrivens and to hell with his stupid wager!

'I'm terribly sorry,' said Mousie unhappily, breaking the silence at last. 'I've done something wrong, or said something to upset you.'

'Of course you haven't, don't be silly,' he snapped at her. Then, hardly any more gently, 'What do you want to do, then? Put on another record or something? You came to listen to records after all, didn't you?'

'No...I think I ought to be going...' She was almost in tears from the sudden and unexpected brusqueness of his manner. 'It's later than I realized and I'm on duty first thing in the morning.'

Churlish in his resentment he watched in silence as she took her coat off the peg on the back of the door, and struggled into it.

'I'd better walk you back to the nurses' home.'

'There's no need. We're right on the edge of the hospital grounds and it'll only take me a minute.'

'It's no trouble.'

'*No*...Really. Thank you. I'll be quite all right.' Her voice had a note of angry firmness he had not heard before.

'Look, I'm sorry if—'

'Thank you for a very good meal. Good night.'

'Good night.'

After she had gone he turned his record-player on full blast until neighbours thumped on the walls. He washed the dishes in his cramped little handbasin, managed to break one of the glasses in the process and cut himself collecting up the pieces.

And when Charlie Wootton dropped round bringing a half-bottle of whisky in his overcoat pocket, he was told in no uncertain (but extremely clinical) terms what he could do with himself and his nightcap.

CHAPTER TEN

Janet Dunbar faced her operation the next day with mixed feelings. She was nervous at the thought of what lay ahead of her, but delighted at the prospect that at last her problems were going to be dealt with in a positive way; an end to the pain and the uncertainty and waiting around and being endlessly nagged to drink and drink when she was not thirsty.

It seemed a long night in spite of the sleeping-pill they had pressed her to take, and she was not even allowed an early-morning cup of tea to help her to pull herself together. By the time the day nurses came on duty she was feeling generally low and distinctly apprehensive.

Staff Nurse Miniver, who came to prepare

her for theatre, did not really seem her usual cheerful self either, but Janet was in no mood to speculate why.

'Your husband rang a few minutes ago, Mrs Dunbar. He said to tell you good luck and keep your chin up.'

'Will he come in this evening?'

'I suggested he didn't, because you'll still be very sleepy after the anaesthetic, but he'll telephone again instead.'

Janet tried not to show her disappointment. It was obviously sensible, after all. How silly to feel suddenly lost and homesick.

'You'll see him tomorrow, you know.'

'Yes, of course.'

Janet's spirits sank lower as the curtains were drawn round to make a little private rectangle, then her own pretty nightie was taken off and replaced by a drab anonymous theatre gown and her hair bundled away under a turban which made her look more as if she was going out to do a morning's cleaning than a patient on her way to theatre.

'Never mind, you shall have your own

things on and your hair brushed as soon as you are properly round again afterwards,' promised Shirley. 'Now I have to check that you haven't got dentures of any sort. No. Good. You've still got your identity label on. Any jewellery on! No, your wedding ring's all right; in fact, we tape it on with a bit of sticking plaster, like this, to be sure you can't lose it. I'm afraid the next thing is that all your make-up has to come off. Don't look so startled, it's for a good reason. The doctors, particularly the anaesthetist, have to be able to see the colour of your skin, particularly your lips and your nails; it's one of the main guides to the state of your circulation.'

'I didn't know that,' said Janet. 'Actually,' she confided, 'I spent ages this morning doing my make-up and varnishing my nails as the only way I could think of to keep my courage up. So this is a bit...well, demoralizing. The last straw, as it were.' She laughed, rather shakily.

'I'm awfully sorry. I've never thought about it like that before. What you look like doesn't really make that much difference, does it?'

'I don't know how most people feel. But I think it does. Knowing you look your best gives you self-confidence. Like having nice clothes. Anyway, it's fun. What time am I going to theatre?'

'I don't know. You're second on the list. so I'm going to get your pre-med now, then I'll leave these curtains round and you'll find yourself going quite drowsy, not worrying any more, and even having a bit of a sleep.'

She was right. A pleasantly euphoric weariness followed the injection, broken some three-quarters of an hour later by the curtains being rattled violently open by the theatre porters with their trolley.

'Here we go again then, eh?' She was jolted sharply back to reality.

She edged her way across on to the trolley, clutching her modesty blanket firmly round her. One of the junior nurses was detailed to accompany her down to the theatre, Staff Nurse Miniver gave her an encouraging wink, and the group started on its way.

'Hey steady, Jock,' said the nurse as the trolley bumped against the swing doors of the ward, so that Janet raised her head, startled, to see what was going on. Not that she cared much: the pain was back again, and bad.

'Take it easy, will you, you actually chipped a bit of the tile going round that corner. Are you all right, Mrs Dunbar?'

'I...think so. But if you could slow down a bit...'

'Oho, so you two ladies, don't like my driving, eh.' he did a neat four-wheeled drift to end up in line for the next lift, almost dumping Janet on the corridor floor, vanity blanket and all. 'Well, I've never had any complaints before.' Clang against the lift gates. 'And I've taken more patients to theatre—' bump against the side of the lift and Janet winced— 'than you, little nurse bossyboots, have had hot dinners.' Crash against the far gates so that the whole king-size lift juddered. And as a final mark of his contempt for life in general, he slammed the big gate across with such ferocity that Janet thought it must break.

Suddenly, with that last jolt, Janet became aware that something odd had happened. The pain had stopped. That pain, her old friend and enemy that had lurked and pounced and succumbed for short spells to injections only to reassert itself again, faintly or overwhelmingly but always there: it had gone, completely and dramatically. There was not even the lurking ache she had come to think of as being pain-free, nothing except a strong wish for a bedpan.

She started laughing.

'It's gone, Nurse,' she said. 'The pain. It's gone.'

'Yes, dear. Your pre-med would stop it hurting.'

'No, I don't mean just made it go farther away and be bearable, like with the drugs and injections, I mean really gone. Do you think I could possibly have a bedpan?'

They were just going into the outer

vestibule of the operating theatre and the little nurse was obviously embarrassed by the mis-timing of this request.

'Well, they don't have any bedpans on theatre. Besides, they see to all that for you before they actually start operating, you know.'

'Please,' Janet pleaded. 'There must be one somewhere. I might have to wait a few minutes, and I'm desperate.'

A sympathetic anaesthetics nurse appeared, and from somewhere, eventually, the necessary article was produced. A few seconds later Janet passed it back gratefully. But she hardly expected the excitement it caused.

'You've done it!'

'Congratulations!'

'Talk about the nick of time.'

'Someone tell the surgeons.'

What was all the excitement about, Janet asked the little nurse who accompanied her.

'The stone! You've passed it! You won't need the operation after all.'

'But that's marvellous! You see—you thought I was mad when I said the pain had stopped.'

An imposing figure in green gown, cap and theatre mask and white wellingtons which made Janet want to laugh by their very incongruity, came striding out of theatre pulling at his rubber gloves as he walked.

'Well, young lady, I'm told you've done me out of a job this morning,' he boomed. 'Well, come on, girl,' he turned on the nurses, 'where's the evidence. I don't take things like this on trust, you know.' He examined the now-celebrated object closely.

'You've got a good sense of timing, Mrs. er...'

'Dunbar, Sir Reginald,' prompted one of the nurses.

'...Mrs Dunbar. What did you do? Go over a bump in the corridor on the way to theatre? Everybody laughed dutifully. It was obviously a rhetorical question, but Janet and 'her' nurse looked at each other, and the porter suddenly had urgent things to do in the sluice.

'The pain's gone?'

'Yes. Quite suddenly, just before we got along here.'

'Just like going to the dentist, eh?' Sir Reginald was, to everyone's relief, in good form this morning. He might on other occasions, just as easily have swung off at all and sundry because good operating time was being wasted. 'Well, at least you've saved yourself an ugly scar under your bikini. Has the next patient been sent for?'

'Yes, sir.'

He nodded to Janet and disappeared back through the theatre doors.

The ride back to the ward was, oddly enough, relatively smooth, with Janet clutching what she proudly called Exhibit A in a small glass specimen jar.

'This is wonderful news, Mrs D.' Staff Nurse Miniver was genuinely pleased.

Dr Doyle, who had escaped from his duties on theatre for a few minutes, and, still like some stocky wood sprite all in green, followed them to the ward to give instructions for the remaining patients to be premedicated early, and Janet herself kept under observation, added his congratulations.

'There's only one thing I want now,' said Janet.

'What's that?'

'Some breakfast, please.' Everyone laughed. 'And then a long sleep.'

The first idea presented no problems; the second was more doubtful—Margaret Llewellyn, approaching down the ward, saw to that. No one had told *her* it was operating day (and it was a bit late to tell her now) and as ever her timing was impeccable.

With Janet now safely in bed, houseman and staff nurse, by common consent, turned away and started up the ward towards the office.

'Good morning, Mrs Llewellyn,' they said, nearly in unison like a comic stage act, striding on to safety before either could be trapped again.

'Is Saturday still OK for you, by the way?' asked Bill once they were safe.

'Well, yes, but are you sure...?'

'Why not? They're free tickets, after all. The woman's obviously a nut case, but if she wants to go round distributing good things to poor and needy hospital staff that's up to her.'

'All right, then.'

'See you, then. Back to the blood and guts meanwhile.'

' 'Bye.'

And Margaret commented: 'Don't they make a *nice* pair?' in a smug tone to Janet, as they watched the green theatre gown and the trim white and blue uniformed backviews walking briskly together up the ward, before she went on: 'And how are you? My dear, I simply must tell you about my plans for next year's Friends of the Hospital Garden Fete. I've managed to get Lady Harrington-Firbright to open it—you know dear Pamela Harrington-Firbright,

I'm sure...'

Getting out of hospital was not going to be the only good thing about going home, reflected Janet gratefully.

CHAPTER ELEVEN

There was no doubt about it, Jamie told his shaving mirror the following Saturday, the evening was shaping up to be a one-hundred-per-cent-bore. How on earth had he come to let Selina bulldoze him into taking her to Matron's Ball? It was ridiculous. Matron's Ball was notorious as being about the squarest event this side of the equator and even the idea of fancy dress as an innovation seemed typically old-fashioned.

But Selina had nagged and Selina had bullied. And when Selina had two free tickets, and a spoilt little pout of her crimson lips because she felt neglected recently, her nagging and bullying could wear down any poor man who wanted nothing more than a quiet life.

He had given way with good grace simply for the sake of peace and quiet. He had even, more from disinterest than good nature, allowed her free choice over the costumes they would both wear. Her strange sense of humour had lighted upon a monk's habit for him, and he began to struggle into it now, hating the idea more every minute. The wig turning his full head of hair to a lean tonsure gave him nasty twinges about what his mirror would see in twenty years' time or so, and the brown habit and cloak seemed to be made from the leftovers from a blanket factory suggesting that he would be in a walking oven for most of the night.

He had come to some sort of terms with the outfit by the time they arrived in the ballroom, tying his rope girdle in a fancy array of knots, and raising a few mocking wolf-whistles by a nifty manoeuvring of the skirts to show an impressive expanse of blue sock, old leather sandal and hairy shin as they went up the staircase. The ballroom was the enormous nurses' common room, as big and normally as bleak as a barrack square, but tonight magnificently disguised with balloons and streamers, the stage covered with tiers of plants and flowers and transformed into the bandstand where a noisy squad with huge monograms all over everything were already giving tongue enthusiastically. The high french windows were open on to the enclosed lawn between the staff canteen and the nurses' common room, normally a scruffy defoliated quarter-acre where off-duty nurses dried their hair or studied on sunny afternoons off; but tonight made magic by rows of coloured lights swinging in the night breeze.

Jamie's immediate instinct to find the bar and stay there was, predictably, firmly vetoed by Selina, and he settled with a resigned sigh for buying them both drinks and finding free places among the line of tables round the walls. They found one of the last empty tables left, and congratulated themselves on having chosen their arrival time well.

All round them Harlequins and Columbines sipped drinks, Lone Rangers danced with Elisa Dolittles, Che Guevaras flirted with Minnie Mouses. A Pearly King was having his buttons counted by a Viking maiden with long blonde woollen plaits; and a court jester at the next table was comparing details of headdress with a clown in broad hoop-topped trousers and shoes which flapped heavy soles as he walked, and which he loudly assured everybody he had been wearing round the wards right up until the previous day. Across the room a Charlie Chaplin had started the evening badly by overplaying his part and spilling a glass of wine down the front of a magnificent lilac crinoline whose lace-capped wearer was not amused.

'Some of the costumes look dashed hot,' said Jamie. 'At least I shan't be the only one to suffer.'

'At least you can relax in your costume,' said Selina, giggling. 'That's more than I can in mine.'

It was no less than the truth; for Selina's costume was a Bunny girl, fractionally, invitingly, intentionally too small, so that wherever anything was designed to fit to her curves it fitted just a trifle too closely. For every bulge of hers there were several bulging pairs of male eyes at the tables round them. Her boyishly-cropped black hair was sleeked down and matched admirably with the black and white of the suit. Generous breasts curved to alluring advantage straining against the black satin that (more or less) imprisoned them. Broad, defiant hips, a pert perfect roundness of a rump (what gluteal muscles!) with its ridiculous little white bunny's scut, and the whole turnout perfected by those long legs in their black fishnet tights and high-heeled shoes. She sat now, one knee crossed over the other and the free foot swinging provocatively in his direction as she sipped her drink. His for the taking.

Such vamping was usually well enough to his taste, and it accorded well enough with the image he had so long enjoyed building for himself that the most blatently sexy woman in the room should so obviously be laying claim to him. But perhaps he was tired. Somehow she did not appeal to him quite as much as usual. It occurred to him, as it had never consciously done before, that perhaps Selina lacked a certain subtlety of approach, that her giggle was just a little too high-pitched and too frequent, her voice too loud. She was good fun, OK for a laugh, first class for a bit of slap and tickle. He (and most other males in the hospital) knew that. Was there, he wondered, anything she actually cared about, anything she had even thought about long enough to sit down and talk about it? Perhaps that body, glorious as it was, especially now in its bunny-girl splendour, was all there was of her. Perhaps if you were to pick her up and shake her she would rattle, or the flesh case would crack and she would shower broken springs and ratchets and levers all over the ballroom floor. (And some earnest registrar would dash forward to write it all up for some learned journal

246

of anatomy, thought Jamie.) And just the high disembodied giggle would remain.

How would *she* look in a simple woollen dress? he wondered. Good, of course. Definitely good. But she would hang it about like a Christmas tree with heavy clinking jewellery, anodized baubles and coloured beads. Never a simple chain just visible under the wool...

'Hey, come on, lover. Stop day-dreaming and jog me round the floor a few times. There's plenty of time later on for what we all know is going on in your masculine mind.'

He got up, hitching his robes into the girdle as best he could before holding out his hand to her. She wiggled to her feet and started to dance close to him, a little closer than strictly required by the steps of the dance. She was wearing a popular and much-advertised perfume. It was not one he liked very much.

'Hey, look at Andy Pandy,' drawled Selina, undraping herself from round his neck for long enough to point out a radiologist they both recognized, wearing an elaborate blue-and-white striped suit ornamented with white rick-rack and white woolly bobbles. 'Did you ever see anything so ridiculous? He's even got make-up on his eyes and cheeks.'

'So have you.'

'That's different.' She was in a singularly humourless mood this evening.

'He must have gone to a lot of trouble over the costume anyway, or somebody must.'

'Can't imagine why he bothered, it's a disaster,' she decreed, her bright expertly-made-up eyes darting round the room for the next victim to destroy.

An Archbishop of Canterbury swept by, regal in gold cloth and purple, mitre at a slightly tipsy angle as he danced with Dick Whittington's cat who held her tail up as elegantly as any long dress as she waltzed.

'Her whiskers are coming unstuck already,' noted Selina gleefully. Then, 'I say, wasn't that Dickie...whatsis-name?'

'The Archbishop? Yes. Dick Vincent from orthopaedics.'

'Hah! From what I've heard that costume's the closest *he'll* ever come to godly living.' She added, after a pause: 'Mind you, there are those who would say the same about you and your monk's garb—not that I, for one, am complaining.' She gave him a sensuous squeeze to make the point of her remark quite clear.

Very gently he extricated himself from this over-proximity. Warm female flesh, well arranged and scantily clad. All he could ask for. Usually. Nothing fragile or mysterious or precious about her. None of that sort of nonsense. Just as well, too. And yet...there was a word for Selina this evening, if he could remember it...'

'What's the matter with you, for God's sake?' she asked, puzzled and annoyed. It sounded more like 'fer gawd's sake', Jamie noted uncomfortably.

He murmured some excuse about being too hot in his costume.

'Hot?' drawled Selina. 'brother, *you* are about as hot as a frozen halibut.'

He remembered the word he was searching for: Overkill. It summed Selina up perfectly.

He muttered something about being tired.

'It doesn't usually make any difference,' she pouted, deliberately dancing close enough to rub herself against him.

Hell, the guy was actually backing a step away from her. In this costume. Every other man in the room would have been eating out of her hand by now. What was up with him? Was he sickening for something? Well, if he wasn't reacting like he should, perhaps she'd better try cutting her losses. There were plenty of other fish in the sea and the night was still young. Just over there, for instance, was that rather interesting Bill Doyle who had been chatting her up at some length when he was in the office a few days ago collecting his complimentary tickets in exchange for some sort of voucher written out by old Bossy Llewllyn herself. He was man enough to appreciate her in this costume and he looked as if he needed rescuing from that drab little nobody he was with.

'Look, Selina, I'm sorry...' Jamie somehow had the feeling that life nowadays was spent apologizing for crimes he did not wholly understand.

'It's all right, Jamikins,' she said brightly, patting his cheek. (How he wished she would not use that awful name.) 'I've an idea, why don't we join up with someone? Brighten the evening up. I've just seen that nice Dr Doyle across the room, and there are two empty chairs at his table.

'I don't really know him...'

'*I* do. Come on. Bring the drinks.'

As they threaded carefully between the crowd of costumed figures jostling each other at the edge of the dance floor, Jamie could see Bill, looking as bored as he, Jamie, felt. He was draped in a white sheet with black bone shapes ingeniously attached to it to form a skeleton. A death's-head mask hung by its elastic round his neck as if he had just

251

taken it off. Only when they were nearly to the table and Selina had launched upon her joyous greeting of Bill, so that a belated retreat was out of the question, did Jamie realize who Bill's partner was, and his heart slipped in a couple of extra half-beats from embarrassment and something near to panic. Shirley Miniver was the one current problem in his life to which there seemed no acceptable solution, and he had counted on keeping well out of her way until he had one worked out.

Bill, brighter by the minute, was carrying out expansive introductions. Already, in the first few minutes, his arm had found its way round Selina's waist once, and he did not look exactly loth to resume the sortie.

'Hallo,' said Shirley.

'Hallo, Shirley,' said Jamie, carefully putting the drinks on the table and sitting down.

She was wearing a Scandinavian peasant-style dress, with a simple black dirndl skirt of heavy black taffeta embroidered near the hem in green and red and decorated with a pattern of tiny beads. The top was a bolero-style waistcoat encrusted with whirls of beads, held with a criss-cross of laces down the front, over the simplest loose white muslin blouse gathered into soft ruffles of tatted lace at the throat and cuffs. On her head was an embroidered juliet cap. There was something about the ornate simplicity of the whole effect that matched Jamie's idea of her completely.

'I like your costume,' he said.

'Thank you. Yours is good too. It must be terribly hot to wear, though.'

'Yes.'

What would otherwise have been the longest, most embarrassing pause in either of their memories was filled by Selina and Bill gleefully dissecting the costumes passing them on the dance floor. The height of cattiness was reached on the subject of Miss Gray, who, dressed with unparalleled un-suitability as Cleopatra could have qualified for a special prize, had there been one, for the drabbest costume of the evening. If ever velvet drooped, if ever rampant snake on gold headdress failed to ramp, if ever jewelled ornaments hung determinedly crooked, it was on the unfortunate Miss Gray.

'Either age has withered her, or custom has staled her infinite variety,' commented Bill drily. Selina looked at him as if he was mad.

'What *are* you talking about?' she said.

'Just another way of saying it would need a pretty hungry asp to fancy her.' Selina was not much the wiser but giggled obligingly anyway.

Or a pretty hungry Prince Albert to fancy *her*, thought Jamie as the lilac-crinolined Queen Victoria loomed out of the crowd a few yards away, hacking her way through the tangle of bodies, apparently intent on reaching their table. The composed smile on her face was further devastating evidence that she intended to fraternize when she got there. Bill's reflexes acted with commendable promptness.

'Quick! Dance!' he commanded Selina,

grabbing her by the wrist and launching himself towards the floor with her, surprised but not unwilling, in tow.

Shirley was almost as quick, though somewhat less precipitous.

'I don't usually do the asking,' she said. 'But this is an emergency. Will you dance—quickly?'

Obligingly Jamie got up. The lilac Queen reached them at the same moment.

'Hallo, Miss Blandish,' said Shirley, with apparent pleasure. 'You never mentioned you were coming tonight. Do you know Dr McTweed? Jamie, I'm sure you've heard me speak of Sister Blandish.'

'How do you do, Miss Blandish,' said Jamie politely. 'Actually we were just on our way to dance; you will excuse us, won't you?'

Once they were safely round the dance floor once or twice, Shirley started giggling quietly.

'I'm ashamed of myself, really,' she said. 'But really I couldn't face another dose of *her.* Not on top of being on duty with her all day. Though I suppose really we should have tried to be nice to her. She didn't seem to have anyone with her, perhaps she was a bit lost and looking for a familiar face to latch on to.'

'Well, she's *not* latching on to *us*,' said Jamie firmly. 'You acted with commendable promptitude, Staff Nurse. I shall see your behaviour is reported in the proper quarters.'

'You mean you'll actually tell Sister about me...sir?' Shirley began to giggle again. It wasn't a giggle, though, not in the irritating abrasive way that Selina giggled; it was a quiet, infectious bubbling up of humour which made him want to laugh too. He did, and, without even realizing it, they both relaxed.

There was another pause in the conversation, but no longer an awkward one. Her hands were cool, not flabby but pleasant to hold. Her lips were probably cool too, he thought, invitingly cool like earthenware on a hot day.

'I was very rude the other evening, wasn't I?' he said, after they had done another round of the floor without speaking. 'I didn't mean to be. I'm sorry.'

She looked down, suddenly as shy again as she had ever been. 'No, you weren't. I'm sorry if I made you angry. I'm not very used...'

She coloured and he felt a rush of sympathy for her. He felt too a sort of protective possessiveness towards her. There was probably nobody, he thought, nobody else in that room who knew as he knew what an incredibly beautiful girl she really was. Nobody who had seen that soft brown hair curving on to her shoulders or the way her eyes could sparkle in soft light or the dimples...oh, those bewitching dimples... and yet, there they were, still, just the same. Now he knew about them he could see them even with her hair tortured back into its combs and the owl-eye spectacles killing every feature. It was a good secret, his secret, no their secret—Shirley's and his.

In those few minutes as they danced, she was hardly even aware how closely he was looking at her for she was busy watching the other people round them. He realized just why he had been so angry with her, so put out and consequently so rude. And why he had used circuitous corridor routes to avoid her for the past few days, eaten away from the hospital and generally gone to considerable lengths not to see her. And the realization, now it came, was totally devastating. And the most wonderful thing in the world.

'Shirley,' he said. 'I think I'm in love with you.'

'Sorry.' She grinned back at him. 'It's that fellow showing off on the drums. I didn't catch what you said.'

'I think—' he realized he was shouting. He stopped and grinned back at her (yes, there were the dimples, plain as anything, teasing him). 'I think I need a rest from this energetic dance. Shall we sit out for a bit?'

She nodded, and laughingly indicated a

quiet corner away from where Blandish was last seen. He, however, steered her towards the french windows, and they walked together out into the still evening.

In contrast with the brash noise of the dance floor the quiet was overwhelming. Neither of them spoke, but their hands met and held, as if each had by common consent been reaching for the other.

'God, Shirley, but I'm a stupid idiot,' said Jamie at last. She did not say anything but looked at him in surprise, eyebrows arched questioningly.

'I've been in love with you for nearly a week, and it's taken me till now to realize it. Oh, sweet, sweet Shirley, I love you, I love you so much. That evening...all those glib, stupid things I said to you...they were just...nothing. Now that I really know what I want to say...Oh God, the words just get in the way...'

She had turned half away from him while he was speaking. Was it because she was moved by his words or because she did not share his feelings and found his stumbling efforts distasteful or embarrassing? he wondered.

He had never felt so uncertain of himself, or such an idiot in all his life. He had heard and read that love could do this to a man. He had never believed it before. Now all that made him stand his ground was the certainty that she, if anyone in the world, would understand.

After what felt like an hour he summoned courage to reach out and turn her face very slowly towards him. She did not resist. In the light from the coloured bulbs hanging round, he saw that there were tears in her eyes.

'I love you, Shirley,' he said again. 'I love you...Oh, I...'

But she was in his arms. Her soft lips were against his, as cool as he had imagined but alive with passion too, provoking warm excitement in all his body as he held her close to him.

'Do you...could you...feel the same way

about me?' he asked her at last.

There were still tears in her eyes, but she was laughing even while she brushed them away.

'Oh, Jamie,' she said, 'of course I love you—I think I've loved you all my life. Only I never, never dared dream...'

He took her two hands and held them tenderly against his cheeks, then softly opened the fingers to kiss each palm in turn. Then, magnetized and mesmerized by a look he had never seen in her eyes before, he let their linked hands fall softly and they stood joined, for a moment and for ever, by the eloquence of that glance.

'I love you, Shirley Miniver,' he whispered.

'I love you, Jamie McTweed,' she whispered back. And they kissed again, as softly and gently as the touch of a butterfly's wing.

Where did the rest of that evening go? They could not have told you, afterwards. Perhaps they joined the noisy crush again and danced happy in their own quietness together in spite of all the bustle round them, their own still point in a turning world. Perhaps they even danced with other people, like Bill and Selina, but their eyes were only for each other even across the packed ballroom, with a magnetism so tangible you would think anyone who broke the beam would have been aware of it. Perhaps they simply stood in the cool under the coloured lights, unspeaking for long moments at a time, for although there would be plenty to say later, at leisure, the magic now was too strong for any need to talk—fingers intertwined or arms gently round each other (even their own restraint seemed to bewitch them) looking at the dark sky and the stars.

'Jamie,' she said, 'all my life I have been lonely. Now, already I can't even remember what it felt like.'

He held her to him, easing his monk's cloak round her slim shoulders in the chilly night.

'I promise you'll never be lonely again,' he said.

One day not long after this Shirley tried a new hairstyle, still as tidy as ever, but a little looser around the ears, and somehow allowing the hair itself to circle and soften her face. Drawing courage from the evident success of this she tried her hand at make-up, aided and abetted by Janet Dunbar the morning before she went home.

A week or so later Jamie went with her to give moral support when her contact lenses were fitted. He was rewarded by walking out of the optician's with undoubtedly the prettiest girl in Titchford on his arm for all the world to see.

The secret's out now, he thought. Everyone can see how wonderful she is. But it doesn't matter any more. They're all too late. She's mine and mine alone. And he kissed her proudly, there in public for all the world to see. They were on their way to choose an engagement ring.

Shirley looked radiant on their wedding day, ethereal with white satin and lace and happiness. Jamie did not need any of the back-slapping congratulations to tell him how lucky he was: he could not take his eyes off her.

It was a splendid occasion, or so he was told afterwards. He was too nervous to remember very much about it except the sea of feathery hats and finery, carnations on morning coats, endless champagne, hand-shakes, good wishes. And Shirley, his Shirley. *Mrs* McTweed.

There was one thing he would not forget in a hurry, though. And that was Bob Scrivens, so-called best man, who, unspeakable wretch, came sidling up behind him just as he and Shirley were about to cut the tiered wedding cake to mutter in his ear in a hoarse stage-whisper:

'My God! The lengths some people will go to just to win a simple bet!'